Pretty - A fairy Tale Retelling of the Frog Prince

The Crown and the Sceptre, Volume 5

Kristina J Jordan

Published by Kristina J Jordan, 2021.

This is a work of fiction. Similarities to real people, places, or events are entirely coincidental.

PRETTY - A FAIRY TALE RETELLING OF THE FROG PRINCE

First edition. November 9, 2021.

Copyright © 2021 Kristina J Jordan.

ISBN: 979-8201799397

Written by Kristina J Jordan.

Also by Kristina J Jordan

The Crown and the Sceptre
Free A Fairy Tale Retelling of Rapunzel
Strong - A Fairy Tale Retelling of the Princess and the Pea
True A Fairy Tale Retelling of Puss in Boots
Pretty - A fairy Tale Retelling of the Frog Prince
Loyal - A Fairy Tale Retelling of Red Riding Hood

CHAPTER 1

Roaring fire blazed high, hot flames seared lush green grass and coated the air with an ashy pallor.

Auber coughed on thick smoke as he wriggled into the unpleasant, cool, sticky mud. He shuddered at the unpleasant slimy sensation. He blinked, watching the soaring castle towers blacken and crumble.

The castle was Auber's home; he'd never been outside the boundaries of Lord Ruben's estate. He sank deeper into the mud, gazing at the blinding flames that licked the darkening sky; ribbons of orange and red laced in swirling smoke. Lord Ruben had been inside the castle when the fire started; Auber felt a pang of guilt and sorrow. Although Lord Ruben was a terrible father, he was the only father Auber knew. Cruel and heartless at worst and negligent at best, he was still Auber's flesh.

Therese croaked as she flicked a fly out of the air with her tongue. "Serves him right," she said without apology. Her voice matched her looks— dark and throaty.

Auber blinked again, holding back his revulsion. He never could get used to eating like a frog. Since the change, Auber usually hopped to the kitchen, nosing for scraps, but there would be no scraps now. The castle kitchen reduced was to cinders. The staff fled days ago when Lord Ruben strode into the castle kitchen in a thundering rage, throwing a curse at Auber. Poor Therese had been standing mixing her delicious ginger cake and when Lord Ruben's lack of experience and control sent the curse flying astray, she bore the brunt of it; taking on the tastes and mannerisms of a frog as well as the amphibian appearance. There was no chance of reversing the curse now because the only way to undo Lord Ruben's curse was mutually falling in love. Knowing full well Auber had no access to social connections, Lord Ruben had informed him of this gleefully after plopping him and Therese in the lake adjoining his castle.

How Auber would convince someone to fall in love with him, when he wasn't actually himself, was a mystery, let alone how he would help Therese, his loyal childhood friend. Auber sank into the murky water, now speckled with ash and grit from the fire. Maybe he could find some lotus seeds; they would at least be more palatable than flies. He eyed Therese as her long pink tongue snapped another insect from the smoke laden air.

****

The fire was still glowing two days later. Auber dragged himself out of the lake, hopping clumsily toward what remained of his former home. Maybe there would be some scraps, something that could help him escape this horrible fate. A shadow passed through the cloudless sky. Auber glanced up, heart thudding in a panicky rhythm. Even after months of being a frog, he still forgot the sky was often as dangerous as land or water. An unmistakable creature swooped overhead, grey scales covering a tough, leathery hide. Auber cowered into the reedy grass, wishing he hadn't left the lake.

The dragon was joined by another; equally huge, it could have squashed Auber with a single toenail.

"Mildred, we fully destroyed Lord Ruben's castle last week. I told you that yesterday," the first dragon said, turning to his reptilian companion with an irritable edge to his voice.

"I know, Hugo, but there's magic here. I feel it. Lord Ruben was up to something," Mildred, the second dragon, answered. Her colossal head wove back and forth, golden eyes scanning the gardens and the lake.

That's right, dragons feel magic, Auber thought. He'd always done his best to avoid magic; his father had shown him it brought nothing good. Ever. But maybe dragon magic was good. Maybe the dragons could help him reverse the spell. The thought struck Auber like a bolt of lightning. If the dragons could undo this horrible spell, he could be human again. Human and free from his father. A thrill of excitement ran through his body.

Auber hopped forward, toward the speckled dragon, Mildred.

"Excuse me, Mildred?" Auber said, voice croaky, but clear.

Mildred ignored him, continuing to squint her great golden eyes.

"Mildred?" Auber said, louder this time.

"Auber? Auber, what are you doing?" Therese splashed from the lake, water and mud sluicing from her deep green skin.

"I'm getting help. Don't you want to be free of the curse?" Auber asked, turning to his companion.

"Auber, I know Lord Ruben was your father, but as long as that awful man doesn't exist anymore, I am free," Therese replied.

Auber hopped clumsily toward Mildred. "Come on, Therese, maybe these dragons can help us escape these frog skins. Don't you want to be human again?"

"Of course, I do.... But...." Theresa answered, her voice filled with doubt.

"But what?" Auber kept hopping, determined to get the creature's attention.

"You might be right, Hugo," Mildred said. "The magic here is so faint. We must have destroyed most of it. The rest will fade on its own. You know these spells never last long after their makers pass away."

Auber froze.

What was that supposed to mean? Was Auber going to die soon, or was the curse going to fade?

"I feel sorry for the poor creature, whatever it is," Mildred said, flicking her long tongue.

"I am the poor creature," Auber shouted, speeding up his pace, with Therese in pursuit. He had almost reached the dragons. Just a few more feet until he reached Mildred. His webbed feet scrabbled for purchase on the loose soil as leftover smoke burned his lungs.

"I'm here," he shouted at Mildred.

Hugo shrugged. "At least we got to stretch our wings. We should fly here more often; the views are fantastic." He unfolded his colossal wings, flapping for takeoff.

Auber realised the dragons were leaving him on Lord Ruben's estate. Alone on the estate, in the most forgotten corner of the Lovanian kingdom.

"Hurry, Therese, come on. It's our only chance." Instinct kicked in. With a desperate leap, Auber surged forward, grabbing the dragon's huge toe and clinging for his life. He glanced behind him. Therese was closing in, dark eyes bulging with effort as she strained upward. Auber stretched out his back leg, letting Therese use him as a ladder to clamber beside him.

Just in time.

They crouched low, clutching the hot scales as the dragon flapped its huge wings. Cold air whistled around them, sharp and crisp. Auber's stomach lurched as they left the ground.

Stark, cold horror enveloped Auber as he looked down. Tiny green balls spread underneath like a tufted carpel. Trees, he realized with a sickening heave; the thick forest covered the rich Lavonian soil. A patchwork of fields peppered the land with lighter greens and yellows. Lord Ruben's holdings were extensive, with land and mines. Gold and copper, Auber gleaned from the paperwork Lord Ruben left littered around his study. Lord Ruben cared little for his holdings, only visiting often enough to fill the spaces with a increasing array of magical treasures and artifacts. Auber shivered. It was a kindness the dragons had done by burning that wretched place down. Lord Ruben's castle stank of evil.

CHAPTER 2

Auber and Therese clung to the dragon's claw, fear choking Auber as they were swept along.

Cold air whistled as they soared through clouds toward dazzling sunlight. Being a frog, Auber didn't feel the cold, but his muscles stiffened as the dragons flew on. The only saving grace was their hot dragon skin warm against his belly.

Finally, when Auber's muscles cramped and his eyesight blurred from the stinging wind, they slowed, descending through the clouds. Auber gulped as he braved a glance down. The dragons were heading toward a double peaked mountain peak. Grim, grey rock. The dragon slowed, lumbering to a halt in front of a rough doorway chiselled into the rugged mountain face.

The dragon's lair.

They landed with a thump. Clumsy and stiff, Auber tumbled from his perch as Therese plopped nearby, stumbling on a loose stone.

"Where are we?" Therese said, blinking as she accustomed herself to new surroundings. Rocks littered the bare ground, grey stones replacing the lush green grass, the reeds, and the placid lake at Lord Ruben's estate.

"The dragon's live there." Auber hopped toward the deep, dark opening yawning before them—black against the bright sunlight.

Therese shuddered. "I'm not going in there."

"It's our only hope," Auber answered.

The dragons were shaking their massive wings, folding them back into their bodies. Mildred ambled toward the opening.

"I guess we should check on the egg," Mildred called over her shoulder. A puff of smoke drifted from her nostrils and Auber had to hold back a sneeze as the smell of sulphur floated through the air.

"Come on," Auber said, ignoring the smoke to hustle after Mildred. One of her steps equalled about forty of his, so it was hard work keeping up.

"I can't believe you talked me into this," Therese grumbled, hopping after him. "There better be bugs in there. Because I'm starving after all that flying."

Auber and Therese slipped in the doorway, following Mildred into a flat, sandy cave. Auber's eyes nearly popped out of his head at the sight of gold littering every available surface. Careless piles of coins, gold bars, and gems were scattered along walls; even Therese hesitated, murmuring under her breath.

Mildred and Hugo ignored the gold, stepping over it to head toward one of the many doorways cut into the back wall.

"Hello, Quinn," Mildred said, her raspy voice crackling into a high-pitched cooing. "How's my little eggy?"

Another dragon popped its head out of the doorway. "Eggy's well; we were just having a singsong. How was Ruben's estate? Everything gone?"

"Mostly." Mildred stuck her nose into the doorway, admired something just out of Auber's eyeline. "There are vestiges of.... something. I'll fly back and check next week and see if I can learn more."

Quinn sniffed the air. "I can smell magic on you. Are you sure you didn't step in something nasty Lord Ruben left lying around the grounds?"

Mildred sat on the floor, lifting each giant clawed foot to give them a beady eyed examination and a cautious sniff. "No. Hugo, check your paws; Quinn smells magic on us."

Auber shrank behind a gem studded chalice as Quinn's nose twitched at each giant clawed toe.

"This one." Hugo wrinkled his nose and wriggled the toes of his left hind foot, the foot Auber and Therese had journeyed on. Mildred leaned down, her giant nostrils grazing the floor.

"Phew, that's definitely Ruben's magic. It reeks," she said, then coughed, sending a shower of sparks skidding across the floor.

"I suppose I'll have to go wash my claws," Hugo complained, holding his foot off the floor and hobbling to another door. Auber heard the faint sound of rushing water drifting from its dark interior.

That must be the dragon's water supply, thought Auber, tucking the information away. Auber knew he would need water to survive. Even now, he felt his skin drying, exacerbated by the windy flight. He exchanged a glance with Therese who glared at him. Apparently, he was not forgiven for dragging her away from her precious lake... and flies.

Auber shrugged, letting his eyes wander around the dragon's den. Now that they had adjusted to the dim lighting, details were emerging. The dragons must have made the den themselves, digging it out with their massive claws; Auber's eyes scanned the grooves marked in the rock. Therese was also taking an interest in her surroundings; although, hers lay in the flies circling the room, their lazy buzzing sound drawing her greedy eyes like a magnet.

Snap. Therese's tongue zipped out, snatching an unsuspecting fly as it hovered over a diamond choker. Quinn whipped his head around.

"Did you hear something?" Quinn asked Mildred, a suspicious expression darting through their great golden eyes.

"No," Mildred said, her own reptilian eyes scanning the room.

"I have a feeling someone's in here. And that icky magic smell hasn't gone away with Hugo. In fact, the smell's getting stronger," Quinn said, testing the air with his tongue while weaving his giant head back and forth.

Mildred joined him, putting her nose to the ground. Auber edged inside the chalice, pressing himself against the inside of the bowl. His heart was thudding so loudly he was afraid the dragons would hear it.

Did dragons have good hearing? Auber wracked his brains, trying to remember.

"Ah ha!" Mildred said triumphantly. "I've found it." Auber peeked around the edge of the chalice, his stomach dropping with a sickening lurch. Mildred had pinned Therese to the sandy floor with a single enormous claw. "You're one of Rueben's magical monstrosities, I can smell it," Mildred said. "Now tell me why you 're here lurking and spying."

"I'm not spying," Therese answered, her voice high and thin, frantic eyes darting toward Auber. "I just wanted to escape that horrible estate. I promise. I'll go down the mountain right now if you free me."

Mildred narrowed the yellow eyes, smoke leaking from her nostrils. "Not so fast. I don't know if I trust you yet."

Therese closed her eyes. "I wouldn't do anything to you. Ever."

Auber stepped—or rather—hopped forward. "It was me," he said.

Mildred's head swung around. She lifted her paw from Therese, flicking her claws in dismissal. "You? You are Ruben's servant?" she said, her dragon voice filling the cave.

"No, not Lord Ruben's servant. His son."

The moment the words slid from his mouth, Auber knew he'd made a huge mistake.

CHAPTER 3

Mildred's huge golden eyes narrowed to angry slits as fiery sparks shot from her nostrils.

"His what?" Mildred's raspy voice roared.

Auber sprung back as a burst of white-hot flames singed the ground where he'd been standing.

"His son," Auber said, his voice a tiny squeak. "But can't you see, he cursed me? Why do you think I'm a frog? I'm Lord Rueben's victim too."

Mildred sat on her haunches, cocking her head.

"Explain, and make it fast."

"My father is Lord Ruben. Sort of. My mother was a servant in his castle; she worked in his herb gardens. Until I came along."

Mildred cocked her head to the side. "Then what?"

"Then... I guess Lord Ruben decided a son would be useful. He was fascinated with magic and hoped I would follow in his footsteps so he kept my mother at the castle; she raised me, secretly. He didn't care too much for me, but he did make sure I was trained by very expensive tutors."

Mildred huffed, but Quinn frowned. "Then where does this other one come into the situation and why did your father turn you into frogs, dearie?" Quinn asked.

"Ru—Father liked to experiment with magic on me. He'd siphoned magic from a shifter, and he didn't want to put his own precious hide at risk. So he used me. Therese and I were in the kitchen together and she got in the way—the curse hit her much worse than me. We can't shift back on our own; the magic has... conditions." The words rushed out of Auber's mouth.

"Oh ho. You'd better hurry and figure it out then. Your window for reversing won't last long now that Lord Ruben's not in the picture; I'd give you a month at the most." Mildred breathed, sending a blast of hot air skating across the sand.

"And who exactly is your comrade?" Quinn jerked her head toward Therese, who was currently eyeing a circling fly.

"Therese, my friend from the castle. She's Lord Ruben's baker who worked in the castle kitchens; my childhood friend."

"A pastry chef," Therese said, puffing out her chest. "You always forget what an amazing pastry chef I am—was."

"Fine," Auber said, rolling his eyes. "You're the best pastry chef. Your ginger cake is out of this world scrumptious. Happy?"

"But what about your mother?" Mildred asked.

Auber gulped. "Mother... died. She was working with one of Lord Ruben's dangerous plants and her glove ripped."

Mildred tilted her head, an almost sympathetic expression crossing the reptilian features. "A plant meant for one of Ruben's concoctions?" she asked.

Auber nodded, the lump in his throat preventing further speech.

"Well. I suppose the fact you 're trapped in frog bodies is our fault. We should have searched the premises more carefully before burning it to a crisp. Lucky you were in the lake because you'd be toasted otherwise," Mildred said, exchanging a meaningful glance with Quinn.

"So can you help me be human again?" Auber asked, excitement rising in his chest.

"Not exactly," Quinn said. "We can't break curses ourselves. But I suppose we could show you how to break it. What kind of ward did Lord Ruben use?"

"A love ward," Auber answered.

"Hm..." Mildred scratched her colossal head with a massive claw. "That's a tricky one. Easiest to create, hardest to break."

"Probably why Father chose it," Auber grumbled. Lord Ruben had a petty streak and loved making things difficult for those he considered beneath him.

"Don't worry about breaking the ward right now. We'll discuss it and get something sorted. We just have to find someone to love you. Should be easy. Humans are fickle creatures," Mildred answered.

Quinn choked back a cough.

"Don't be like that Quinn; people love all sorts of things nowadays. You'll see dear." Mildred said, whirling to shoot a glare at Quinn.

Even through the raspy dragon voice, Auber heard the hesitancy in Mildred's tone.

"Do you mean they have to love me in frog form?" Auber's heart sank as he glanced at his rubbery green limbs.

"Yes, but you'll be fine as long as you remember not to tell them about the estate you inherited. They have to love you, not your property or wealth. The estate would confuse the poor creature."

"What about her? Can you help Therese too?" Auber asked, nodding toward Therese, who was licking her lips after swallowing another fly. Ugh. Auber shuddered.

"I suppose. It might be harder if she doesn't put the effort in. On the other hand, if your father linked your curse to hers, we would only need to break your ward," Mildred answered, wincing as Therese burped.

"What are we doing? What curse?" Hugo asked, emerging from the back of the cave, rivulets of water rolling from his grey scales.

"We brought two stowaways from Lord Ruben's estate," Mildred explained. "We're helping them break the ward Ruben put on them."

"What, those little frogs?" Hugo's nose came within inches of Auber. Auber cringed back from the dragon's fiery breath.

"Ruben shifted them, and they can't shift back. Apparently, our friend Ruben was doing some sort of experiment with a love ward. Even worse, Ruben was that one's father, can you imagine?"

"Horrible man; of course we'll help," Hugo said.

"And that's not all we discovered," Mildred continued. "That one." She pointed a claw at Auber. "Is Ruben's son."

"Ahh…" Hugo's golden eyes widened imperceptibly as he studied Auber and Therese.

After a heated discussion, Mildred decided the dragons would find a suitable target. One who would fall in love with Auber thereby breaking the curse for both him and Therese.

"Don't I have to love them back?" Auber asked, a twist of worry clenching his stomach.

"Don't worry about that dear," Mildred said, waving a claw. "We'll choose someone lovable." Mildred grinned at Quinn, her dragon features contorting into an alarming grimace.

Great, just great, Auber thought, watching Therese flicked her tongue, snatching a fat beetle meandering toward a pile of gold ingots.

****

Finding someone for Auber to love and fall in love with was no simple task. Over the next few days, the dragons flew far and wide, searching for a suitable candidate, but returned to the cave glum and discouraged every evening. Aubrey's heart sunk lower and lower each night. He was afraid to ask about the time limit on his curse; the thought of being stuck in his amphibious form forever made him shudder. But judging from the dragon's uneasy rumbles, the situation wasn't good. The thought of being trapped in his hideous frog body, forced to eat flies and beetles for the entire rest of his life, appalled Auber to his core.

He was comfortable enough; the dragons provided him with a nesting area in the underground river. Therese loved it; dragons attracted plenty of flies with their appetite for meat, and the river was free of predators. Auber suspected Therese would be happy to stay in her frog body forever, avoiding the drudgery of a hot kitchen.

But Auber wanted more; he longed for his human body. Eating human food, sleeping on soft beds, learning. He really missed the learning. Studious Lord Ruben, despite his failings, had provided Auber with an excellent education. Auber's head was crammed full of facts. History, geography, science, history, politics, magic—especially magic.

Auber shuddered, burrowing into damp sandy soil. A vibration sounded in the cave entrance. A thud and a whir of giant wings retracting. Auber closed his eyes, accustomed to the sounds of the dragons' comings and goings. Next to him, Therese grumbled in her sleep— eyes twitching behind dark, leathery lids. Dreaming about flies.

****

"Violette. Violette!"

Her father's voice pulled Violette's attention from the painting she was working on. She sighed. Arel must be on an errand. She would have to answer the door herself.

Violette wiped the worst of the paint from her fingers and flung the door open to see King Abelaird smiling at her.

"Violette, darling, did you forget we have a council meeting to attend this afternoon?" King Abelaird asked, his brown eyes crinkled with worry as he took in Violette's state of disarray.

"Sorry, Father. I was just preparing," Violette said, tossing her long, dark hair and shoving paint smeared hands behind her back. "I was waiting for Arel to help me dress; she'll be here soon."

"That's all right, darling; I'll get someone to send her now. But please hurry, I like to get to the council meetings first," King Abelaird said with an indulgent smile.

Violette closed the door, leaning against it. "Another boring council meeting, sweet boy, so I'll have to get Arel to walk you," Violette said, stroking her hound dog. Brane licked her hand in agreement, always happy to accept his mistress's attention.

After pouring Bane fresh water, Violette strode to the dressing room. If Arel didn't arrive soon, she would have to get ready for the council meeting herself. Father was a dear when he was happy, so Violette planned to ask for a new horse soon. Lady Merry had a beautiful dapple-grey mare, as fast as wind and Violette hated being shown up when pleasure riding. Violette frowned, examining a row of colorful silk dresses. She discarded the red; father's council members were old-fashioned and it would be wasted on them. Violette settled on a conservative high necked blue, highlighting her blue eyes. She stepped into it, fumbling with the laces. Where was Arel?

A soft knock sounded at the door before it cracked open, a cautious head peeping around the corner.

"There you are, Arel." Violette sat at the vanity. "Hurry and lace my dress while I start the hair. It needs to look good because I have to attend another council meeting."

Arel nodded, expert hands pulling the laces tight.

A few minutes later, a perfectly coiffed Violette swept toward the council room; she would be late, but that's all right; it never hurt to make an impressive entrance. She ran her hand over her smooth curls.

Father's council sat around the long, polished table. All ten members were there. Violette smiled her most brilliant smile, gliding to her seat— a special one covered in jade velvet with lilies and birds carved into the wood. She glanced around the room, hesitating. Something didn't feel right. Every council member avoided Violette's eyes; even Lord Dukek, one of the younger council members who seemed to sometimes value Violette's opinion, refused to meet her eyes. Violette placed her hands in her lap, a slight frown on her pretty features; things would be all right. They always were.

King Abelaird cleared his throat. "Shall we begin?" he said, his deep voice filling the room.

"First order of business," Lord Ravelle began, "the coffers."

Violette pasted an interested expression on her face as she let her mind wander. Not the coffers again. Father's council always complained about the coffers. It didn't seem to make much difference what they did; they would never have enough money to compare to surrounding kingdoms. Luixe had little to offer—no rich mines, scanty agricultural lands, and few skilled artisans. They always seemed to get along fine. Violette always got jewels, clothes, and horses when she wanted them; their table was rich and varied, and father had a lovely seaside estate for Violette to spend hot summer days in.

"... an alliance seems the best course of action," Lord Ravelle said, his voice droning in Violette's ears. Violette tuned out again, wondering why father insisted she attend these meetings. The meetings were so boring; King Abelaird could reign for years before Violette would need to rule the kingdom.

A quiver went round the room as the sentence ended. Tension. Violette noticed it just as her attention was jerked toward her Father.

"An alliance is out of the question," King Abelaird insisted. "As my sole heir, Violette is needed here."

"But what if she marries a second son or a duke; then she could return to Luixe and rule, just richer. There are plenty of estates in Lovan and Iaisia. We'll send someone to investigate, see who's available. Prince Landry, perhaps?" Lord Dukek said, setting his jaw.

Violette narrowed her eyes at Lord Dukek. "I refuse to be bartered like a pony," she said in an icy voice, sliding a nervous glance to King Abelaird.

King Abelaird set a comforting hand over Violette's. "No one will barter you, dear; you'll still make the final choice regarding whom you marry. But the council is right; we need to start thinking about who will rule beside you one day."

Violette rolled her eyes, hiding her growing concern with a flick of her shiny hair. The truth was, Violette had heard this discussion before; what she wasn't familiar with was her Father's acceptance of her impeding marriage. Were things really that bad? Violette racked her brain. True, the crops weren't wonderful and the artisan work had trickled to a standstill. Worse, Iasia's new fleet of ships had put a significant dent in trade. The once bustling routes were reduced to a fraction of what they'd been in their heyday. But surely, surely her Father wouldn't sell her off to the highest bidder.

Violette peeked at King Abelaird; his fingers were laced in front of his chin, his left eye twitched imperceptibly. Cold chills ran up Violette's spine.

Father was serious.

That was the expression King Abelaird used when attempting to talk Violette into something. Usually, it was a boring history lesson, meetings with the trade guild—the list went on. There were quite a lot of royal duties Violette didn't particularly care for.

Violette leaned against the soft velvet, mind racing. If only she had paid attention earlier in the meeting; she could have headed them off. Violette didn't particularly care for the idea of getting married in the near future. Father had ruled alone for years, ever since Violette was tiny, and everything was fine. She didn't mind admirers; she had plenty of those and enjoyed them immensely. But tying herself to one person. Ugh.

She glanced at King Abelaird again, noticing the deepening lines around his eyes and mouth, exhausted by mounting cares and responsibilities. *Maybe I should help more*, Violette thought, a pang of guilt niggling through her. It wasn't like she didn't care about the people of Luixe. She just didn't think about their overwhelming needs on a daily basis. That was Father's job.

"Violette, are you willing to at least look at a selection of suitors?" Father asked, breaking Violette out of her reverie.

"Fine," Violette said, sighing and crossing her arms in front of her chest. "But only consideration. I decide who to marry and when to marry. You know the law." She gave the council a hard, triumphant look. According to Luixian law, Violette chose her own marriage partner. And she intended to hold the council to that law.

"That's all we need," Lord Tiernan said. "We'll present the selection at the end of the week."

Violette's shoulders relaxed. They said the end of the week, but Father's council took forever to make decisions. If she were lucky, they could discuss potential suitors for months, buying Violette valuable time to invent excuses explaining why those suitors were not suitable. She held back a smile, letting her mind wander again.

After several more articles of business— all which sailed straight over Violette's head— the moment the meeting was adjourned, Violette sped down the hall, eager to return to her room and see Bane.

"Violette?" King Abelaird called.

"Yes, Father?" Violette answered, spinning around.

King Abelaird caught up to her, panting with effort. "I was wondering if you would accompany me to my study for a moment."

"Of course, Father," Violette said, hesitating. Father reserved his study for serious conversations. What was this about? She'd already agreed to accepting suitors.

"Sit," Father waved Violette toward the settee. Violette perched on the edge of the brocade seat, watching as King Abelaird sat behind his desk, a polished work of art carved from a single piece of wood—a gift from one of the Southern Kingdoms.

"Violette, I should have shared this with you earlier, but I haven't wanted to alarm you. The truth." King Abelaird paused, pouring amber liquid from a cut glass carafe. "The truth is... Luixe is in a sticky situation financially."

"Sticky situation, you mean we're poor?" Violette asked, squeaking out the last word.

"Not... poor. But not as rich as we were. And there are several important expenses coming up. We need to cut back our spending."

"Cut back our spending?" Violette repeated the words dumbly, trying to grasp the meaning.

King Abelaird cleared his throat, fiddling with his glass. "Maybe not quite so many jewels and dresses this season?"

Violette rubbed her palms on the skirt of her dress. "Yes, Father," she answered in a small voice.

King Abelaird swallowed his drink. "It's only temporary, dear. It's just the navy; the ships need repairs..." his voice trailed away.

Violette stared at her hands. How could a few measly dresses possibly pay for an entire fleet? Even she knew that was a mere speck compared to their needs. She thought guiltily about the jewel boxes in her dressing room stuffed full of baubles. Father had never complained.

"So, it's good we had this talk." Father's cheeks were red. He stood, dismissing Violette.

Violette drifted down the corridor in a daze. Poor. How could this happen? She went back to her room, patting Bane politely when he poked his cold nose into her hand. She pressed chilly hands to her hot cheeks. Did everyone know? Was she the only one who hadn't realised they were in dire straights. She thought back to all the council meetings she attended, council meetings she avoided by letting her mind wander to more pleasant subjects. Violette sat at her dressing table, staring at her reflection.

At least she was pretty, shiny dark hair, smooth creamy skin, a delicate nose—just the right size and shape. She absently dragged a comb through her hair. Maybe she would have time to finish her painting before dinner. That would clear her head.

"Miss?" Arel entered, feet whispering on the plush carpet. "Shall I help you prepare for dinner?"

"Yes. I'll be wearing the red silk tonight."

At dinner, Violette sipped from her goblet, letting her eyes study the room. Now that the truth was out, she could see the signs. Fish from their own rivers, not imported like before. Fewer guests, only two kinds of wine. Violette's eyes drifted to her father; King Abelaird smiled warmly. Violette gave him a weak smile back. She realised the council was right. Father was right.

Violette would have to choose a suitor.

CHAPTER 4

Violette stared out the window, half completed embroidery abandoned in her lap. One of her duties was to meet the courtiers for afternoon tea.

"We should go for one last summer picnic before the weather changes," a feminine voice sounded in Violette's ear.

Violette jerked her head. "Pardon?" She turned to the speaker, Rose, the blonde daughter of a duchess.

"You haven't listened to a word I've said this afternoon," Rose scolded, setting down her needle with a pout.

"I'm sorry, Rose; I have a lot on my mind," Violette answered. She turned her blue eyes to Rose, pasting a wide smile on her pretty face. "You were saying about a picnic excursion? Sounds lovely."

Violette had settled in one of the spacious downstairs drawing rooms. The French doors opened into the garden, letting in the scent of lilies. Rose wasn't a terrible companion; Violette sneaked a glance at Rose, who was regarding her with an expression of concern. False, no doubt. Violette knew Rose viewed her as competition for the best suitors. *If only Rose knew the council is selling me to the highest bidder,* thought Violette, tightening her grip on the needle.

It had been a week, and Violette had received no word from the council regarding her list of potential suitors. Since their conversation in the study, King Abelaird had been distant, only seeing her at meals. Violette regarded this recent development with cautious suspicion. If things were that bad, the suitor wasn't forgotten, just delayed.

Violette threw Rose a polite smile. "I'm sorry, I had a bit of a headache this afternoon."

"Oh, dear." Rose pasted a sympathetic expression on her pink lips. "I have a wonderful healing oil Sophie recommended to me. Would you like to try it?"

Violette picked up her embroidery, stabbing the needle into the cloth. "That's very kind of you."

A rap sounded at the door as a uniformed maid entered, presenting a message on a silver tray. Violette accepted the parchment, sliding her manicured finger under the wax seal.

"Is everything all right?" Rose asked, eying the message with ill-disguised curiosity.

"Another council meeting, nothing to worry about." Violette thrust the message into her embroidery bag with shaking fingers.

Rose slid Violette a suspicious glance as Violette's cheeks reddened. Violette quickly picked up her embroidery again. "You were saying about a picnic?" she asked, hoping to distract Rose with a subject change.

Half an hour later, Violette locked the door to her chambers and drew the message out of the bag, studying it carefully. The list wasn't long. Twelve names in total, none from Luixe; father's council must be desperate for outside funds. Violette scanned the list, noticing Prince Landry was at the top.

Prince Landry would be a good candidate, Violette thought, running her finger across his name. Prince Landry of Iasia was a second son, so he could live in the Luixian castle and rule beside her. In addition to the royal holdings in Florin, his family owned an extensive estate in Iasia; their wealth would make a substantial contribution to the frequently mentioned coffers.

Violette hastily scanned the remainder of the suitor list before tucking it away. The council meeting was taking place in a few minutes, and she needed to have a plan.

"Prince Landry is clearly our first choice. We thought we'd organise a diplomatic visit to Iasia," Lord Ravelle said, his dry voice droning in Violette's ears.

"Won't that make the Iasian's suspicious, sending me on a sudden diplomatic visit?" Violette asked, feeling like a slice of meat served on a platter.

"That's the point," Lord Ravelle replied in his toneless voice.

Ahh, so she *was* a slice of meat served on a platter, Violette thought, forcing the pleasant expression to stay on her face.

"So I go on the diplomatic visit to Florin?"

Lord Ravelle nodded. "Yes, and of course the listed Iasian suitors will be in attendance. We'll make our intentions clear; all you have to do is look pretty."

Violette slid her eyes to King Abelaird, his hands were threaded on the table, and he avoided meeting Violette's eyes by staring at them with a look of intense concentration.

Realizing her father couldn't help her, Violette sighed. "All right. When do we leave?"

CHAPTER 5

Auber prodded Therese, who responded by grunting and worming deeper into the slick mud. Therese had discovered a tiny patch of slimy mud in the sandy embankment and adopted it as her new home, refusing to move for anything that didn't involve food.

Fortunately for Auber, he hadn't been forced to resort to a diet of flies and bugs while residing in the dragon cave. Not yet. The dragons hunted frequently, returning with plenty of meat. Roasted meat, to Auber's great relief. He couldn't say much for dragon cooking skills. The meat was often charred and never seasoned. But, at least, it was cooked. He eyed Therese as she belched, cracking open a lazy eye.

"What now?" Therese said in a complaining voice.

"Therese, the dragons asked to speak to us," Auber said, poking Therese again, harder this time.

Therese heaved herself from the mud, reluctance etched in every motion. "I suppose we could see what the dragons want," she answered, hopping toward the doorway.

The dragons had generously assigned Auber and Therese a quiet spot on the underground riverbank. Auber would have preferred a nice soft bed with a feather duvet, like he'd enjoyed in his room at Lord Ruben's estate. But dragons weren't individuals Auber cared to complain to, so he kept his thoughts on their living situation strictly private.

"Come on." He hopped into the dragon's center room. Mildred and Hugo were resting on the sandy floor and Quinn lay half burrowed into a bed of gold coins. Quinn shifted as the frogs entered, sending an avalanche of coins spilling across the floor.

"There you are, little ones. I hope the accommodations are acceptable? Enough to eat?" Mildred asked.

Therese and Auber carefully skirted out of range of their giant nostrils to the edge of the cave; Auber had gained enough experience with hot dragon breath by now to realize things could get extremely hot very fast.

"Our spot on the river is fantastic." Auber decided not to mention that cold sand wasn't his first preference. It wouldn't do to offend the dragons, especially dragons who were his sole hope of ever being human again.

"Ahem, wonderful, well we have exciting news," Mildred said, clearing her throat.

"Good news?" Auber asked, perking up his frog ears.

Mildred blinked, scaly skin folding sideways across the golden eyes. "Some of its good," she answered.

Auber's heart sank. "Some?"

He glanced at Therese, who had lost interest in the conversation, fixing her attention on a moth flitting through the cave entrance.

"First, we've thoroughly investigated this curse—er ward," Mildred said, quickly correcting herself. "It seems there's a sticky problem."

Auber felt the disappointment churning in his gut as he waited for Mildred to continue.

"Apparently, Lord Ruben's ancestors had royal blood," Mildred said.

This was news to Auber, and an interesting fact, but Auber didn't understand what royal blood had to do with his frog skin problem.

Mildred slid Auber a significant look, expecting a more dramatic reaction.

"Why does it matter if I have royal blood running through my veins?" Auber asked.

"If you have royal blood, it means only a person of royal blood can break the ward," Mildred answered.

"Oh," Auber answered. That did change the situation, because the only princess living in Lovan was Celine. Judging by the way she and Prince Alex cozied together when they arrived at Lord Ruben's estate, Celine was not a viable option.

"But..." Mildred said with a dragonish grin that showed rows of dagger sharp teeth. "We found a suitable princess for you."

"You did?" Auber asked, relief and apprehension mingling in his voice.

"Of course, we found you the lovely Princess Violette," Mildred said, preening her giant tail with pride.

"Princess Violette of Luixe?" Even from the confines of Lord Ruben's remote estate, Auber heard rumors of Princess Violette filter through. Beautiful, vain, silly, and extremely independent. Someone like Violette would expect—no demand—to be wooed properly. Preferably with jewels, handsome looks, romantic gestures and dramatic gifts. Auber cast a doubtful glance at his slick, green skin.

"And more excellent news. Violette's travelling to Iasia on a diplomatic visit, so all you have to do to break Lord Ruben's curse is allow Princess Violette to find you and fall in love."

"But how? I'm not human," Auber said, gulping. His voice sounded plaintive, even in his own ears.

"Well, you can speak; she'll figure out your human. You'll be fine as long as you don't mention the estate," Hugo said, flicking his sharp claws together.

Auber scratched his head with a webbed foot. "If Violette's travelling to Iasia on a diplomatic visit, isn't she looking for an Iasian suitor like Prince Landry?"

"Weeelll... I suppose. You'll have to hurry be first. You know they'd never let a frog inherit your father's estate."

Auber sniffed. He had little interest in Lord Ruben's estate, especially now that the castle was a smoking ruin.

"Your father's estate isn't just the castle, you know. It includes the mines, farmland, and forests. Your father was one of the richest lords in Lovan."

"What am I supposed to tell Princess Violette?" Nerves clutched at Auber's chest.

"Do something nice for her; human women love that," Quinn suggested, yawning and flexing his claws, digging deep grooves into the sandy floor.

Auber sighed, his shoulder slumping. He knew he should be happy. The task just seemed so monumental.

"Well... if you want to stay a frog..." Quinn said.

"No, no, I'll go," Auber rushed to answer. "What about Therese?"

Auber glanced at Therese, who had her eyes half closed, a sleepy expression on her face.

"Hm," Mildred said, hesitating as her golden eyes slid to Therese. "Therese doesn't need royal blood but take her along. There's a pond at the Luixian castle she might like."

"Right then. It's settled. We'll drop you off in Florin tomorrow afternoon." Quinn flicked his tail, sending an emerald necklace slithering across the sand.

With that. Auber and Therese were dismissed.

****

The castle was bustling with a flurry of activity. Dresses made, dresses altered, shoes fitted, jewellery examined, sorted, and cleaned. If Violette wasn't embarking on such a terrifying mission, she would have soaked it in, embracing every moment of attention. She ran her hands down the silvery silk gown she was trying on. Its pearl shine set off her dark hair and eyes to perfection.

"I'll wear this gown to the opening dinner because first impressions are crucial," Violette said, parroting the advice of her etiquette tutor as she twirled in front of the mirror.

The seamstress nodded, mouth too full of pins to answer properly.

"And I'll need a matching wrap, something with a nice trim," Violette continued, eyeing the silver tray of trim and buttons on the sewing table.

"Yes, Your Highness. Let me assist you." A maid rushed over with the tray so Violette could peruse the trims, eventually choosing a delicate beaded lace and showing it to Arel.

"Pardon, Your Highness." A messenger entered on silent feet. "Your father wants to speak to you."

Violette quickly slid into her own clothes before following the messenger down the long corridor. King Abelaird was in his study, waiting for her. Violette sighed, sinking onto the settee. Not more bad news, she hoped, eyeing King Abelaird's face.

"Ahem, good morning, Violette. Thank you for coming so quickly." Father sipped amber liquid from a heavy crystal glass.

"Of course, Father," Violette murmured with a practised smile.

"I called you here to speak to you in confidence," King Abelaird said, leaning back in his chair.

Violette nodded.

"This is between you and me; the council isn't privy to this information."

Violette sat bolt upright. To her knowledge, Father never moved without consulting his council. She wondered what he could possibly have to say.

"It has come to my attention." Father cleared his throat. "It has come to my attention that items have gone missing from the Luixian treasury."

"Missing, as in stolen?" Violette said, her mouth rounding. Only King Abelaird and a few select council members had keys to the treasury. Violette mentally filtered through the council members, wondering who the culprit could possibly be.

"Do you suspect who it is?"

King Abelaird shook his head. "I don't know if it's a council member or if someone has stolen a key. A servant perhaps?"

Violette sank against the velvet, her hands cold.

"What does this mean, when we already had financial problems?" she asked.

"In addition to the hardships Luixe already faces, it means unless we acquire funds or an extremely lucrative source of trade immediately, Luixe will be bankrupt in the next six months."

Six months?

"What did they take?" Violette said, narrowing her eyes. This was more than incidental pilfering.

King Abelaird downed his drink, promptly pouring another.

"What didn't they take, gold, diamonds, jewels. Your jewels were safe, dear; we stored them elsewhere."

Violet pressed her lips together as she pressed a hand to her head, feeling a migraine blossom behind her eyes.

"So, darling, you see how it's crucial you make a good showing to the Iasians in Florin. Obviously, they can't know our.... situation. It wouldn't be polite for them to ask about finances at this stage anyhow. Pretend everything is fine because your people depend on you."

Violette gulped. She had expected the Luixian people to depend on her someday. But not now. Not like this. She met King Abelaird's gaze. "I'll do my best."

****

Finally, the day arrived. The delegation gathered in the courtyard, preparing for their sendoff. Violette peered out the carriage window, wide-eyed. She rarely had the opportunity to travel and was excited to soak in the country. *My last trip as a free woman.* Violette pushed the thought from her head, instead focusing on the task ahead. Tossing her glossy curls, a smile curved her red lips as she waved at the well-wishers sending her off.

People cheered as the delegation slowly creaked through the city. Violette watched from the carriage. From the scene outside, it was hard to believe the Luixians were in dire financial straights. Colourful flag waving citizens lined the streets as Violette waved, never letting her smile slip until they left the gates of the city.

After departing the outskirts of the city, Violette's carriages wound slowly through the countryside. Messengers had ridden ahead to let every Luixian town and village know they were travelling through. Everyone wanted a glimpse of the princess. Violette's cheeks ached from smiling at so many people.

As they left the cities, the villages grew poorer. Violette noticed the children, although happy and cheerful, were ragged, with pinched faces and big eyes. The cottages and farms were tidy, but obviously in need of repairs. Violette's eyes were opened to the state of the countryside.

"Are all Luixian villages like this?" Violette asked, turning to Arel as she pointed out the carriage window.

"Like what?" Arel asked, a perplexed look in her eyes. They were passing a shabby cottage, greyed by time. A ragged boy crouched in the front garden, weeding rows of wilted cabbage.

"So poor," Violette answered, a wrinkle forming between her eyes.

"Things have been declining for years now," Arel replied.

Violette waved, but the little boy didn't look up.

The party spent the night at Wild Rose Inn in Harwulf which was a pleasant three story wooden structure covered with dark green ivy.

"Would Your Highness like a meal brought up?" the innkeeper inquired.

"I'll join the others." Violette didn't care for the innkeeper's obsequious tones and oily manners, but smiled politely anyway. After hours of sitting in the carriage, she longed to stretch her legs and explore the town.

"Is there anywhere I can walk?" Violette asked Arel.

"There's Market Square; if you're lucky there might still be a few venders around," Arel answered.

After picking at a subpar dinner of tasteless stew and hard bread, Violette and Arel set off, accompanied by a collection of guards.

"Which way is Market Square? Everything looks the same in these towns," Violette asked, glancing around as they crossed a cobblestoned lane.

"This way," Arel said, pointing down the dusty street.

Pulling her skirts away from the grimy cobblestones, Violette followed Arel down the main street. A wooden building stood proudly in the middle of the square, a peeling, painted sign announcing its status as the town gathering place. Most venders had left the market, but a few food peddlers remained scattered across the square. Violette sniffed the air, drawn to the smell of fried dough and hot buttery sugar.

"What are those?" she asked, gesturing to a stack of sugar-coated pastries. Her mouth watered.

"Nonnevot, they're a speciality in this area of Luixe. I used to eat them a lot when I was young. They're delicious," Arel answered, steering Violette toward a vender.

The vender was still frying the pastry, slinging metal baskets of dough from the pot before deftly rolling each in sugar.

Violette's stomach growled as she wondered why the pastry chefs at the castle hadn't thought to make these.

"I want that one," Violette said as she reached across the pile, her eyes fixed on a fat golden pastry.

Violette's sudden movement startled the vender, who bumped into the oil vat, splashing droplets of boiling oil into the fire.

A splash was all it took. Instantly, the vat of oil roared into an inferno of flames, reaching red fingers into the darkening sky.

Violette jumped back quickly, but not before the thirsty flames licked the sleeve of her dress.

The next moment was a whirlwind of screaming, searing pain.

Quick thinking, Arel slammed Violette to the ground. Violette's teeth jarred, her face pressed against grubby paving stones as Arel beat out the flames.

Everything went black.

****

Violette inched her eyes open as the room slowly came into focus. Everything hurt. She glanced at her left arm, where swaths of white bandages covered every inch of skin.

She blinked, shoving back knives of pain as her mind struggled for comprehension.

"Where am I?" Violette croaked.

"You're awake," a soft voice spoke behind her.

Violette turned her head, then froze as a dizzying wave of pain enveloped her.

"You're in my cottage. I'm the village healer. Do you remember what happened?"

Violette closed her eyes. "The pastry cart is my last memory." A hot tear trickled down her cheek. Violette longed to swipe it away, but didn't dare move because of the pain enveloping the entire side of her body.

"You've been badly burned; you're lucky your lady's maid knew what to do or you wouldn't be alive right now."

"How—how badly?" Violette glanced at the stark white bandages, fearing what lay beneath.

The healer placed a soothing hand on Violette's good arm. "Now now. We mustn't worry about that now. I've given you the best of care and you'll soon feel better. I'm Fiona, by the way."

"Is the damage... repairable?" Violette asked, terrified to hear the answer to her question.

The healer's brown eyes met Violette's. "My skills can heal them, but I can't bring your skin back again."

Another tear ran down the end of Violette's nose.

"Can anyone heal me?"

"I would to give you an answer, but it's too soon to know." The healer put a cup into Violette's good hand. "Now, drink this; it will help you rest."

Violette took the cup, gratefully letting the cool liquid slide down her throat. It had a strange, bitter taste. She realized halfway through a potion must have been added to the drink. Her eyes grew heavy.

"Hush now." The healer adjusted the pillow under Violette's head.

The next time Violette woke up, she felt better. Lucid. Violette glanced around. It was late; the room was wrapped in darkness, a faint yellow line under the wooden door showing the cottage was occupied.

"Hello?" Violette called, struggling to sit upright.

A swath of lamplight flooded the doorway as Fiona's figure entered.

"Are you feeling any better? I changed your dressings, and it looks like the skin is healing."

"I feel better than before," Violette answered. "I'm a little hungry though."

Fiona laughed. A soft musical note. "Of course. I'll bring you something to eat now." The healer disappeared, returning shortly with a tray containing toast topped with melted butter, a broth full of vegetables and chicken, and a cup of sweet liquid.

Violette nibbled the toast and ate half the broth before she pushed the tray away. Fiona fussed around her, adjusting pillows and blankets before leaving her in the soft darkness.

Violette lay awake, thinking. Fiona's reaction to her injuries told her they were extensive. She took a cautious assessment. Her left arm clearly sustained the most damage, but the stabbing pain in her left cheek and neck worried her. How would she attract a suitor with a deforming injury? Violette hoped desperately the wounds wouldn't scar. But in the meantime, she had decisions to make.

A few hours later, Violette heard the distinctive rattle of carriages rolling down the cottage lane. After a hushed conversation, King Abelaird strode into her room.

King Abelaird failed to hide a grimace when he saw Violette's bandaged form.

"Father?" Violette fought back the hot tears stinging her eyes.

"Violette." Father sat in the rickety wooden chair next to Violette's cot and took her right hand.

"I'm sorry, Father," Violette said, sniffing.

King Abelaird cleared his throat, patting Violette's hand. "It was an accident, darling."

"What about the delegation?" Violette asked, peering at her father through tear-stained eyes.

"We'll delay the delegation until that's—er—healed. We'll send you to Iasia then."

"But how long?" From what Violette suspected about burn injuries, they took time to heal. And she only had mere months to find and marry a wealthy suitor.

"We'll find a healer. The best." King Abelaird patted Violette again on her blanket covered leg.

A thick silence fell over the room. Violette didn't dare ask how much a healer would cost, but she suspected it was more than they could afford.

"The healer says it will be another few days before we can move you." King Abelaird stood, brushing the dust from his breeches.

"You're leaving already?"

"There's a council meeting; I can't miss it," King Abelaird answered, averting his eyes.

Violette nodded mutely, watching as her father swept out of the tiny room. She didn't need to ask what the council meeting was about. Her. Or rather her failure to obtain a decent marriage alliance before she even attempted. Violette turned her face to the wall and closed her eyes.

CHAPTER 6

Auber heard dragon whispers outside the entrance to his watery cave.

He scaled his sandy bed, creeping toward the doorway, then skulked through the shadows, entering the cave's center room where Quinn, Hugo, and Mildred sat engaged in a heated discussion.

"I know what I heard," Hugo insisted. The scales on his back rose into sharp points, a sure sign of dragon annoyance; Auber had discovered this through close observation.

"I know you're there, Auber." Mildred sighed. "Come join us; after all, this does concern your issue."

"It does?" Auber left the shadows, hopping across the sandy floor.

Mildred nodded her huge, scaly head.

"There's been a change of plans," Mildred said.

Auber waited.

"Violette isn't travelling to Iasia on a diplomatic visit. She's staying in Luixe."

"Why?" Auber asked.

"It appears the princess had a mishap. Poor human creature isn't immune to fire like we are," Mildred said, sympathy flashing through her huge golden eyes. "Violette was damaged and has to remain hidden until the King Abelaird finds a healer who can get rid of her scars."

"That will make your job easier. Less competition," Quinn said.

Hugo gave Quinn a shove.

"Quinn, the poor little creature is injured. Be nice."

Quinn had the grace to lower his head guiltily.

"Can a healer fix a burn wound without leaving scars?" Auber asked.

"Of course, dear," Mildred answered. "Not in Luixe though, and not cheap. I doubt King Abelaird can afford to import such a healer. Humans are terrible at saving their gold and Luixe hasn't been financially stable lately."

"We leave for Luixe tomorrow night?" Hugo said.

Mildred nodded, already distracted by Quinn, the devoted dragon parent who was returning to the egg nesting cave.

The next evening, Auber struggled into the pocket of a complicated leather harness strapped around Hugo's shoulders. This contraption would be safer and more comfortable than clinging to a dragon claw. Dragons used the harnesses to carry treasure, but they were making an exception for Auber and Therese; Hugo explained as he grappled with the straps.

"I hope this flight doesn't kill me," Therese grumbled, climbing in behind Auber, huddling at the bottom of the leather receptacle, crouching tight against the seam.

Auber squatted next to Therese as Hugo leapt into the chilly air. He was grateful not to see the dizzying height firsthand as the harness swayed in the whistling wind. Three stomach churning hours later, they soared above the Luixian castle under cover of darkness; Hugo swooped silently into the castle garden.

"I'll leave you here." Hugo opened the bag, depositing a queasy Auber and Therese into the reeds. Auber shuddered as the slimy mud squished between his toes. If he ever had his own home, he decided, it wouldn't have a pond.

"The is the most popular section of the castle garden," Hugo whispered. "You should run into Violette soon enough here. Goodbye and good luck."

Auber nodded, watching as Hugo leapt into the sky, a black shadow sweeping against the starry sky.

They were alone. It was up to Auber now.

Auber squished his way across the reeds toward the deeper water, searching for a less slimy place to wait.

The next few days were filled with tedious waiting, and Auber worried the princess would never show up. He saw plenty of people.

Castle staff; trimming, weeding, planting cutting. Auber steered clear of them. He didn't want to be ended like an annoying pest.

The garden was frequently used by castle guests, and Auber listened intently to their conversations. He stayed unnoticed, hidden deep in the reeds, and overheard many interesting things. Interesting but not useful. Auber winced as he got an earful about lady Harrell's latest affair and the price Lord Northalar paid for her diamond necklace.

Apparently, princess Violette wasn't ready to be seen in public. Understandable, Auber wasn't sure if he was ready to be seen in public either. He cast a disdainful glance at his green skin.

It wasn't until a week later, just after sunset, that Auber caught his first glimpse of Violette. At least, Auber thought it was Violette. It was hard to see under the billowing veil and voluminous cape. A companion accompanied the veiled figure. They glided silently across the velvet grass; the orange sky gilded them with light.

Auber sat on a lily pad, nibbling a pile of seeds he collected from the birdfeeder when he spotted the figures. In a flash, he abandoned his meal, diving into the water and swimming for shore as quickly as his flippered legs would move.

He pulled himself into the reeds, through the sticky mud he usually tried to avoid.

"Violette. Violette," Auber said in a croak.

Violette drifted closer to the pond, deep in conversation with the other woman. Not a maid, Auber noted. Now the woman was closer. Her bearing was far too confident, and she appeared to be giving Violette instructions.

"One drop only," the woman said, slipping a small round object into Violette's hand. The object glinted as Violette tucked it into the folds of her cloak.

Strange place to conduct a transaction, Auber thought absent-mindedly, hopping closer to the path, desperate to attract

Violette's attention. Who knew when he'd get another chance to meet the reclusive princess.

"Violette. Violette." Auber was mere feet away, but Violette still hadn't noticed him. He took a deep breath, filling his reptilian lungs.

"Violette." He finally croaked so loud he startled himself.

Violette shrieked and jumped into the air. The small object she'd tucked into her cloak flew out, rolled across the ground, and plopped into the pond with a splash.

"Sorry," Auber apologized, hopping into the path. "I didn't know my voice was that loud; I didn't intend to frighten you."

Auber saw the pale outline of a face under the thick veil as Violette pressed gloved fingers together.

"My salve, it fell in the pond," Violette said, panic edging her voice as she knelt to peer into the murky depths.

"Are you sure?" Violette's companion asked, scanning the long grass beside the path.

"I heard the salve pot fall into the water," Violette answered.

"Maybe it was just a frog, isn't that what frightened you? Here's one right here," the woman said, pointing to Auber.

"Excuse me," Auber said, drawing himself to full height.

"A talking frog? I didn't know we had those in Luixe," the healer said, kneeling to give Auber a closer look.

"I don't care what kind of frog it is, Murele. I've dropped the salve," Violette said, near tears.

The sun had fully set, and only a rim of red light remained at the edge of the sky. Darkness was moments away.

Murele joined Violette. "Are you sure it's in the pond? I suppose I could make more? It would take time because I don't keep the salve ingredients in stock, most are expensive and rare."

"I can't wait. I need the salve now. Father wants the delegation to leave as soon as possible," Violette's voice caught.

"I see." Murele continued to stare into the murky water. "Maybe we could return early in the morning and find the salve. Although, I'm not sure that container will last in the water overnight. It's more decorative than watertight."

Violette sat on the ground and began removing her shoes and stockings.

"What are you doing?" Merele shot Violette a concerned look.

"I'm going to find my salve," Violette answered, setting her shoes and stockings in a neat pile and tugging at her gloves.

"You can't go in that water. It will make the wounds worse."

"Well, are you planning to search the water?" Violette asked.

"I can't swim."

Seizing his chance, Auber cleared his throat. "Pardon ladies, perhaps I can assist you?"

Violette's veiled head turned. "Can you find my salve for me? It's in a shiny round container."

"I can. But I'll need payment. Grant me a favor in exchange for the salve," Auber said, knowing it was a risky move, but unwilling to miss the opportunity.

"What favor?" Violette asked, her posture stiffening.

"Nothing much. Just invite me to live in the castle, like a pet," Auber said, nearly choking at the last phrase.

"Done," Violette agreed without a thought. "But only if you return the salve intact."

"Of course." Auber hopped toward the pond, slithering into the water. By now, it was dark. But not to Auber. His amphibian night vision was second to none. He slid through the water, searching for a flash of gold. The bottom of the pond was a tangle of roots and tree branches. Auber avoided the old turtle, an unpleasant character and very territorial. On and on he searched. Finally, wedged between the roots of a lily, he saw a hint of yellow. He swam down and nudged it. A golden container, perfectly round. The salve.

Auber poked at the salve pot, freeing it from the roots, then grabbed it with his two front feet, cursing its slippery, unwieldy shape. He shoved against the bottom of the pond with his powerful back legs, kicking himself to the surface.

"Here," Auber said, letting the salve pot roll onto the grass.

Violette reached down and plucked the salve from Auber's paws. She wiped the container carefully with the edge of her cloak before clutching it to her chest.

"Thank you." Violette put the salve in her cloak and started putting on her stockings.

"You're welcome," Auber replied, edging closer.

Violette slipped on her shoes and rose to her feet.

"Um.. should I follow you now?" Auber waited in awkward silence as Violette adjusted her cloak.

"Oh, yes. That." Violette paused. "I have a rather big dog... are you sure you need to stay inside the castle? Maybe I could build a tiny house for you here. The gardeners wouldn't mind."

Auber's heart sank. Violette wasn't attempting to wiggle out of her promise, was she?

"No, I really want to stay inside the castle. With you."

"Fine, let me come back for you tomorrow. I'll have to warn Bane or put him in the kennels. I wouldn't want him to eat you," Violette said, fussing with her veil. "Come on Murele. It's getting dark," Violette said, setting off toward the castle; her graceful form melted into the darkness as Auber stood along beside the pond.

So this was how it would be. Auber rested on his webbed haunches. He hadn't expected it to be easy, but it was obvious Violette had little intention of keeping her promise to him. Auber slid into water. Tomorrow, he would take matters into his own hands.

The next morning, Auber woke early. It was hard not to, with no curtains blocking the glaring light. He ate a light breakfast, then went to find Therese, who was lazily sunning herself on a half-submerged log.

"Therese?" Auber said, nudging her sleeping form.

"Huh, what?" Therese mumbled.

"Therese, I'm going to the castle for a while. I'll be back as soon as I can."

"All right." Therese's eyes slid to half mast. "Be careful," she said, closing her eyes again.

Auber set off across the garden.

The castle garden was vast, especially for a creature of Auber's size. Auber struggled toward the main castle. Larger than Lord Ruben's estate, the castle was a massive grey structure that never seemed to get closer, no matter how much effort Auber put in with his tiring frog legs. Finally, he had the luck to spot a cluster of courtier ladies out for a morning stroll. Auber slipped under a large ruffled skirt, wedging himself into the stiff fabric.

"Fifi. Stop," the lady said, shrieking as a fluffy white dog sniffed the hem of her dress. "Lady Finola, control that dog of yours."

To Auber's immense relief, Fifi was collected and scolded by her owner, and Auber didn't see it again. Judging from its high-pitched bark, it was a spoiled lap dog and probably getting carried by its cosseting owner. Auber was jealous; the slippery fabric of the skirt didn't lend itself well as a vehicle.

Fortunately, the ladies soon headed back to the castle. Auber saw the grey paving stones passing under the skirt and slid down, hiding behind a potted fern. When the ladies passed, he peeked out, getting his bearings.

Auber was standing at the entrance to the formal garden, where wide stone steps led to an entrance hall, not a grand front entrance hall, but a comfortable garden room with seats and large French windows. Bookshelves lined one wall. Auber assumed it was a sitting room for cold or rainy days. With extensive effort, he scrambled up the stairs, thankful not to be interrupted, and slipped through the French doors.

Now to find the princess's chambers.

Finding Violette's chambers was a challenging task. Auber wandered endless corridors, heart in his throat every time he heard a sound. It was warm and dry in the castle, and Auber's skin itched from lack of water. He worked his way into a more luxurious part of the castle. Plush rugs, tapestries and paintings decorated the well-lit corridor. *This must be either the guest wing or the royal apartments*, Auber thought, hope flaring in his chest.

A maid rushed by, carrying a tray laden with a silver tea service. Maybe tea for the princess. Auber hopped after her, nearly losing sight of the maid when she darted around a corner. She halted before a heavy wooden door, rapping softly before entering. Auber almost tripped over his webbed feet, sliding inside just before the door swung shut.

"Tea, Your Majesty?" The maid arranged the tea things on a side table.

"Thank you." A deep, rumbling voice answered.

Your Majesty? Auber gulped. This wasn't the princess's chamber. Auber had stumbled into King Abelaird's chamber.

Before Auber could make a hasty exit, the maid slipped out, the heavy door thudding shut behind her.

Auber was trapped.

He stood, frozen, pressed against the wall, desperately hoping King Abelaird wouldn't notice him. He didn't. At least, not until the king pushed himself back from his desk and walked right towards Auber's corner, making a beeline for an ornate cabinet standing against the wall. The king knelt, scanning the contents of the cabinet, as Auber cringed back, trembling. King Abelaird was less than two feet away.

The king pulled out a bottle of amber liquid, eyeing the levels before carrying it to his desk and adding a healthy dollop to his tea. He took a slug from his teacup, letting his eyes wander around the room.

"What's this?" King Abelaird's eyes settled on Auber.

Auber gulped. He was caught.

"How did a frog get it here?" the king said, grabbing a large bowl of carved crystal fruit and dumping out the contents. He approached Auber, intending to pop the bowl upside down over him. Auber hopped through the king's legs, leaping toward the desk.

"I don't think so," King Abelaird said, spinning around. *He is remarkably quick for an old man,* thought Auber, watching the bowl move toward him.

"Wait," Auber croaked. "Just a moment."

The king paused, bowl frozen mid-air.

"Am I going crazy, or did a frog speak?" King Abelaird said, his eyes darted around the chamber.

"I talked. I can talk. I'm a talking frog," Auber said, his heart pounding.

King Abelaird squatted on his haunches, peering closely at Auber. "I haven't even drunk that much. A talking frog in my castle. Fascinating."

"Yes, I'm awfully sorry to bother you. I was actually looking for Princess Violette's chamber," Auber explained.

"Why do you need to find Violette's chamber? You aren't a spy, are you?" King Abelaird asked, his eyes narrowing.

"No. I'm not a spy. Violette owes me a.... favour."

"Stranger and stranger," muttered King Abelaird. "What kind of favor does Princess Violette owe you, little frog?"

"Last night, Violette dropped something in the pond, and I fetched it for her. She said if I found it, I could stay in her chamber. Like a pet," Auber said, stumbling over the last word.

"Ah. I see. So you're holding our Princess Violette to her promise?" King Abelaird asked, face creasing in amusement. "Violette can be quite absent minded, especially lately." The smile slid from King Abelaird's face.

"Yes. It's a lovely pond, but I prefer living indoors," Auber said.

"Well, we must hold Violette to her promise. It would do Violette good to think of someone besides herself for a change. Although, I suppose that's my fault." King Abelaird sighed. "Very well. Hop in; I'll take you to her." King Abelaird held the bowl toward Auber.

"You will? I mean, thank you." Auber hopped into the bowl. The crystal was cold and slick under his webbed feet.

Leaving his tea, King Abelaird took the bowl into the corridor.

"Your Majesty. What happened?" a maid scurried toward them.

"A frog in my study."

"I'm so sorry, Your Majesty. Here, let me take it. I'll see it's disposed of properly." The maid held out her hands for the bowl.

"No. I'll see it. Violette will keep the frog as a pet."

The maid tried and failed to hide the shock on her face. "Yes, Your Majesty." She curtsied, watching as King Abelaird carried Auber down the corridor. He rapped at a door.

"I'm not hungry yet; come back later," Violette answered, her voice muffled by the chamber door.

"It's father, dear," King Abelaird replied.

"Oh." Moments later, the door opened. Violette, in a paint stained dress, stood in the doorway.

"Are you painting again, darling? Wouldn't you like some fresh air?" King Abelaird entered the room. It was stuffy, and the bed was crumpled. Clearly, Violette had painted immediately after waking up.

"Yes, I'll go walking later." Violette rubbed a paint of streak across her forehead, but it wasn't the paint that drew Auber's attention. It was the scar.

Half healed, the angry red mark spread across the side of Violette's neck, creeping up her cheek in spidery lines. Violette's arm was wrapped in bandages, but Auber suspected the bandages hid more of the same damage to the creamy white skin.

King Abelaird scanned Violette's marred skin. "Have you been using the salve, dear?" He asked, a hint of stress behind his mild tone.

"Of course, Father." Violette flushed, making the red welts deepen until they were nearly purple.

It will take more than salve to heal those scars, Auber thought, assessing Violette's injuries, wondering if any healer in existence had the skills to return Violette's scars to the smooth skin that covered the rest of her body. She was a pretty girl—not just pretty—beautiful. Auber realized.

"Ahem, can we come into your chamber?" King Abelaird asked, holding out the bowl.

"We?" Violette asked, peering around her father with panic flaring in her eyes.

"Me and—him. Sorry, I didn't catch your name," King Abelaird apologized.

"I'm Auber."

"You again?" Violette said, sniffing as she opened the door wide for King Abelaird.

"Yes. Me again," Auber answered. "I was explaining to your father about our agreement."

"Agreement?" Violette asked, a tiny wrinkle appearing on her forehead.

"Yes. I fetched your salve in exchange for a place in the castle."

"Oh, that." Violette flopped on a brocade chair. "Wait, you meant you want to actually live in my chambers?"

"I certainly did," Auber answered as King Abelaird set the bowl on the floor and Auber climbed onto the plush rug. So much better than slimy mud.

"Did you make an agreement with... Auber," King Abelaird asked his daughter in a stern voice.

"I suppose I did," said Violette. "Very well. He can stay, as long as Bane doesn't eat him."

"Perfect," King Abelaird said and smiled. A real smile. One that lit up his eyes as he gazed at his daughter fondly.

"Who's Bane?" Auber asked, scanning the room.

"He's my dog. Arel's walking him, and he'll be back shortly."

Auber gulped, wondering how big this dog was; he'd forgotten Violette had mentioned the dog last night.

"Don't worry; Bane's gentle. I'm sure you'll get along fine." King Abelaird dusted his hands. "I'll leave you here then, Auber."

Auber hopped onto a tasselled footstool, watching as King Abelaird exited the chamber, crystal bowl swinging from his hand.

Violette returned to her painting. "I suppose I should have fetched you earlier. Sorry about that. I've not been myself lately," she said, dabbing some pigment onto her palette.

"That's all right," Auber replied, taken aback by the apology. "I've not been myself lately either." He cast a rueful glance at his green skin.

A smile played around Violette's lips. "I guess we're both in a sticky situation; I'm supposed to be looking for suitors." Her smile faded, eyes hardening. "I've tried everything... but nothing seems to make any difference." She glanced at her bandaged arm.

"The salve doesn't work?" Auber asked.

"Probably another useless remedy." Violette waved at the vanity where every inch of the polished surface was covered with bottles and containers. Some simple, some ornate, like the golden sphere he'd fetched from the bottom of the pond.

"You got all those?"

"Yes, people keep telling me to give it time. But I don't have time," Violette said, a bitter edge slicing through her voice. "And, I can't keep buying these useless potions. It's not fair to father.... To the kingdom."

"Do suitors care so much about looks?" Auber asked.

Violette gave a broken laugh. "The ones I need do."

Auber remained silent, realizing he couldn't betray his knowledge about Violette's situation.

"I don't know why I'm tell you this, anyway," Violette said, plucking a loose thread on her bandage. "I suppose you're not part of the court;

they're all watching, and they can't wait to see me fail. Whoever's been stealing from Father's treasury most of all."

"Stealing from the treasury?" Auber asked. The dragons hadn't shared this bit of information.

Violette nodded. "That's why I need to find a suitor quickly."

"Do you know why?" Auber asked.

"Why?" a curious look crossed Violette's face.

"Why, someone's stealing from the treasury. If you know why, you'll learn who it is."

Violette shook her head. "I never thought about why; I assumed father knew the reason."

Auber settled himself. "It might be harder for King Abelaird if the thief is in your father's network. They'll know how to cover their tracks."

"But how else would we learn who it is?" Violette asked.

"Someone from outside the network could be sent to find them," Auber said, puffing out his chest as he realized this was an opportunity to win Violette's favor. "Someone who could slip through the castle unnoticed. What courtiers have access to the treasury?"

Violette wound a finger through her dark hair. "I suppose father's council would be the first place to look. But that's not likely. Father trusts them implicitly. Most of them have been on the council forever... since before I was born."

Auber shrugged. "That's when it gets easy to take advantage of people. Those people stand to gain the most if your father's hold on Luixe fails."

Violette sat up. "Fails?" she asked.

Auber nodded.

CHAPTER 7

"Fails? You think someone is trying to usurp father and take over the Luixian kingdom?" Violette asked, shock and horror flitting across her features.

Auber nodded.

"But how would we find the culprit?"

Auber seized the opportunity to get into Violette's good graces.

"Use me. I can sneak around your castle unseen, and you'd be surprised at the things I've overheard already—and that's just in the gardens."

"You have?" Violette asked, sitting up straighter.

Auber nodded. "I can hide easily, so if you guide me and tell me who to listen to, we'll learn what people say in private."

Violette smiled and clapped her hands, the expression transforming her face. "Let's do it. I've always wondered what people say about me when I'm not there."

Auber shuffled, "Well, I was thinking more along the lines of ferreting out whoever's been embezzling from the Luixian royal treasury.... But we could do that too."

"Oh," Violette said, deflating a little. "Of course. Father has a council meeting tomorrow so I'll take you down early and we'll find the perfect hiding spot."

A bark sounded right outside Violette's chamber. Auber's heart froze in his chest, realizing this must be Bane. He hoped he hadn't made it to the princess's room, only to be attacked by her beloved dog.

"That's Bane and Arel now." Violette ran to the door. "Arel, wait outside with Bane a moment; I'll be right there."

"Quick, we have to find a safe space," Violette said, flitted around the chamber. "Could you stay in this box?" she lifted a trinket box hardly bigger than Auber.

"I'd barely fit in there; I need more space," Auber said, a doubtful expression on his face.

Violette set the trinket box down. "I know." She ran to the armoire. "I keep my dressing gown and things in this cupboard." She flung the armoire open, revealing a spacious interior. Violette shoved aside a row of lacy dressing gowns. "Can you get in there yourself? I'm not used to touching..." Violette's voice trailed away, and she offered Auber an apologetic expression.

Auber hopped to the armoire and clambered inside. Drawers filled the bottom half, which meant Auber was a few feet off the ground. Violette placed a cushion inside.

"There, Arel can bring you food and water later. You don't need insects or slimy worms, do you?" Violette said, grimacing.

"Certainly not," Auber answered. "Regular food will do."

Violette left the armoire door cracked open and Auber peered through the sliver, watching Arel lead a tall, sleek hound into Violette's chambers. Bane sniffed the floor where Auber had been sitting, suspicion present in every line of his lean body. But after whining a few times, he lost interest, wandering to his cushion and curling up with his nose resting on his giant paws. Auber shuddered. Clearly, Violette's dog lived in the chambers. He hoped the creature was well mannered enough not to eat him.

"Arel, could you send for refreshments?" Violette asked.

"Certainly." Arel slipped out, returning a short while later, bringing tea, tiny sandwiches, and biscuits. *Proper food at last,* Auber thought, nibbling at a scrap of ham. The tea was difficult to drink, but Violette promised to bring Auber water later.

"Don't you ever go outside?" Auber asked as Violette returned to her painting. Bane didn't seem inclined to notice him, and Auber decided he couldn't sit festering in a dark closet. Time was running out. He needed to woo the princess now.

Violette sighed. "Not since..." her hand involuntarily reached toward her scarred face. "People don't treat me the same now."

Auber could understand that. He remembered the days when he had been Lord Ruben's son. His father had been absent, but Ruben's castle staff had respected him.

"Well, you'll have to leave, eventually," Auber said in a reasonable voice.

"I suppose. It's just... I was always the pretty one," Violette said, lowering her lashes.

"Why don't you take another evening walk. No one will see you then," Auber suggested, nibbling a crumb of bread.

"Fine," Violette said, sighing. "We'll go for a walk tonight and you'll see what I mean."

Late that evening, a veiled and covered Violette crept out of her chamber. Violette had dismissed Arel for the evening. Dinner was over; the corridor was dimly lit by an occasional lamp throwing pools of yellow light over the carpeted floor. Auber was tucked safely inside a small bag Violette carried. The bag was dark and stuffy; the fabric itched Auber's skin, and he longed to see what was happening.

"Whatever you do, don't swing the bag," Auber said, already feeling queasy from the swaying motion.

"Stop worrying," Violette said. "And shush, I don't want people to think I'm talking to myself."

Violette continued down the castle corridor, taking several turns along the way.

"We'll go to the garden first," Violette whispered. Auber heard a door slide open, then close again.

"Violette, lovely to see you," a honeyed voice said. A woman, Auber guessed the woman was approximately Violette's age. "I was worried you would hide away in that chamber of yours forever."

"Good evening, Lady Sophie," Violette answered in a stiff voice.

"You poor thing, all you've been through." Auber detected a faint tinge of triumphant glee in the feminine voice.

"Thank you for your concern," Violette answered.

"Of course, and please let me know if you need anything. I have the most wonderful healer. She lives near my estate in Donmore. She's wonderful. Why I had a scar... not like yours, obviously. And it cleared up in weeks. Expensive—but that's no bother to you, not with King Abelaird's treasury at your disposal."

"That would be wonderful," a hitch in Violette's voice betrayed her tension. "Send a message to Arel; she'll find the healer for me."

"Of course, darling, and your father? How is King Abelaird coping? He's such a dear," Sophie added in a gushing tone.

"King Abelaird is fine."

"Of course, why wouldn't he be?" Lady Sophie continued hurriedly.

"I really must go, because I am meeting someone in the gardens. Please excuse me." Violette left Sasha. Auber could feel by the swinging of the bag she was eager to flee the nosy Sophie.

"Sophie always asks about Father. The nosy mare probably has designs on marrying him." Violette grumbled. Auber felt a waft of cool air; they were entering the garden.

"Isn't Sophie a little young for King Abelaird?" Auber asked.

Violette humphed. "Of course she is. Sophie's a year older than me. Besides, Father never looked at anyone since..." Her voice trailed away into uncomfortable silence. "Father would never be interested in her."

A faint humming of crickets bled through the cloth of Auber's fabric vehicle as somewhere to his right water tinkled over a fountain; Violette's dress swished as she veered from the path to cross the velvety lawn.

"Violette?" a masculine voice said, interrupting the silence.

"Lord Mihaul," Violette answered. "Are you here for the council meeting tomorrow?" Violette asked, emphasizing the word council. Auber's ears pricked as he listened intently.

"Violette, lovely to see you outside," the voice boomed, deep, but pleasant and friendly.

"Thank you," Violette said. She stopped walking, giving Auber a chance to get his bearings.

"I am here for the council meeting. I trust you're well enough to join us this time?" Lord Mihaul inquired.

"Of course," Violette answered.

"We have much to discuss," Lord Mihaul said, lowering his voice. "Any luck... with the salves?"

Violette flinched as the hand holding the bag trembled.

"Yes, the salves seem to be working."

"Wonderful, we look forward to a detailed report in council."

"Of course," Violette murmured again. Lord Mihaul moved away, and Violette turned and started walking again. Auber felt the cool air disappear. They must be back inside the castle. Auber sniffed the air, realizing this wasn't castle air. It smelled like... hay and manure. He heard a horsy snort. Violette had taken him to the stable.

"Hello, darling."

It was the first time Violette's musical voice lost its guarded tone.

"Sorry I haven't been to see you lately." Auber heard a crunching sound and thought Violette must be offering the horse carrots or apples. Violette moved around the stable, greeting each horse like an old friend.

"You like to ride?" Auber asked as they moved back into the cold air.

"Riding is fine, but I really love the horses because they don't mind me being myself," Violette said.

****

Back in the castle, Auber settled into his armoire. As promised, Arel had brought him a bowl of clear, clean water and another meal. Auber nibbled at a corner of roast meat, better than flies any day. He glanced around the room, taking in Violette's easel. *Princess Violette has talent*, he thought, sipping his water.

"Tomorrow we'll attend the council meeting." Violette disappeared into the dressing room, emerging a few minutes later wearing a frothy nightgown and bed jacket.

Auber watched Violette grow increasingly nervous as the time for the council meeting approached.

"Are King Abelaird's council members that bad?" Auber asked, watching Violette flick through a book, set it down, then return to pacing in front of the window.

"I used to think the Luixian council meetings were boring," Violette said. "But they're depending on me to bring them an alliance. An alliance we desperately need. I don't know if I can do it." Violette glanced at her arm. Today, the princess had securely covered it with a long-sleeved gown.

Auber regarded Violette thoughtfully.

"Isn't there another way?"

Violette drew back the curtain and let it fall again. "Another way? Do you mean find the embezzler then make them restore the treasury? Luixe still needs a powerful and wealthy alliance to prop ourselves up. Luixe doesn't produce much to trade—especially over the past few years."

Auber racked his brain trying to remember everything he'd learned about Luixe from his history and politics lessons. Luixe had some agriculture, little mining, little trade, especially since Isia had expanded their shipping, and they used to specialize in skilled artisans, but the artisans had dwindled in the past generation.

"Why doesn't Luixe build up its artisan workforce again?" Auber asked.

"How so?" Violette asked, turning from the window with a puzzled expression.

"The artisans used to be the lifeblood of the Luixian economy and they've disappeared. Build that trade, give incentives for people to take in apprentices," Auber said. An idea flashed through his mind, spurred by some long ago lesson from a forgotten tutor. "Didn't Luixe used to be renowned for fine craftmanship? Jewellers, silversmiths, woodworkers."

A faint line appeared between Violette's eyes. "I suppose. But... the materials..."

Auber waved a webbed foot. "The materials will come if you provide the skills."

He thought guiltily of his own mines rich with gold, silver, precious stones, and copper.

"But how would I do that?" Violette asked. "Father's council doesn't listen to me; I wouldn't even listen to me. I've spent most of the council meetings lost in my own thoughts."

"Hmm..." Auber cocked his head. "After we attend the meeting today, I'll tell you what my idea."

"All right," Violette said, tugging her sleeve over her hand.

Once again, Violette placed Auber in the little bag. He settled in the bottom. Today, the trip was easier; it was brighter, and he could see shadows and shapes through the cloth. Violette went to the council meeting early to look for Auber's hiding place. Auber didn't fancy sitting in the cloth bag for the duration of the meeting.

"Here." Violette settled Auber inside a potted plant. He crouched under the spreading leaves. *This will do nicely,* Auber thought. He peeked out, noticing he had a view of the entire council chamber. Auber settled back, waiting for the meeting to start.

King Abelaird was the first to arrive.

"Hello, poppet," King Abelaird said, brushing a kiss across Violette's good cheek before sitting in his seat, which was a massive affair of intricately carved wood. King Abelaird poured himself a finger of amber liquid, adding a few drops from a vial he took from his pocket.

"Feeling a head cold coming on," King Abelaird explained, capping the vial and returning it to his pocket.

"Lord Basile," Violette said, enunciating the name clearly as agreed with Auber beforehand. Auber looked out. Lord Basile was a tall, thin man, dour and serious.

"Your Majesty. Your Highness," Lord Basile said, greeting King Abelaird and Violette before sitting at the far end of the table.

One by one, the council members trickled into the chamber. Most members were King Abelaird's age, except the young Lord Mihaul, who greeted King Abelaird and Violette with casual cheer. *Lord Mihaul must be a recent addition to King Abelaird's council,* Auber thought, eyeing the younger man. Lord Mihaul's tall, broad figure matched the booming voice Auber heard the evening before. Auber searched his brain to remember if he'd heard anything about Lord Mihaul's family in his politics lessons. They owned estates, perhaps in the north of Luixe. The memory was vague, sliding away before Auber could pin it down.

Auber peeked from behind his leaf. Lord Tiernan was speaking.

"More cutbacks will need to be made," Lord Tiernan said in a droning voice.

"More cutbacks?" King Abelaird asked, frowning.

Auber watched Violette's slender figure stiffen in her ridiculous green velvet chair.

"But we've hardly been spending anything," King Abelaird insisted. "Why even Violette's contributed. Even with the effort to create an alliance, she's not acquired new jewels or dresses this season."

"Respectfully speaking, King Abelaird, the castle expenses are astronomical. You insist on feeding and housing everyone who breathes in your direction," Lord Tiernan answered.

"We're running a kingdom," King Abelaird said. "You can't expect us to turn people away. Can't we raise taxes? Even a few percent should cover the castle expenses."

Lord Ravelle shuffled a sheaf of papers in front of him. "Taxes are the highest they've ever been. You'll have a revolt on your hands if you raise them any higher. Especially if you intend to continue entertaining at the current rate. The expenditure for last week's ball alone cost enough to repair several ships. The Luixians are noticing the extravagance."

King Abelaird huffed. "Well, you're the Luixian council; if you want to cut back, I expect you to prepare a reasonable proposal. The castle is the heart of Luixe kingdom, and if we don't keep up appearances, surrounding kingdoms will think we're weaklings. How do you plan to make an alliance if we lose respect?"

Lord Ravelle sighed.

"There is also the matter of.... the impending alliance. I hate to bring it up after... the unfortunate situation," Lord Ravelle said, throwing Violette a cautious glance.

Violette's face flushed, her feet shifting under the table.

"We have to wait for the serum to be effective," King Abelaird answered, tension radiating from his voice.

"But how long?" Lord Tiernan asked. "The coffers grow thinner day by day; we need an answer."

Violette spoke, her voice clear and confident. "I have obtained the best salves from healers around Luixe. What else do you want? I can hardly attract a suitor in this condition."

Several of the Lords looked uncomfortable as an awkward silence fell, thick and heavy, across the council chamber.

King Abelaird cleared his throat. "I realize we're stuck in a tricky situation, but Princess Violette is doing her best. We can't ask any more from her in these—er—difficult circumstances."

"Well, I do have one idea. We could we host suitors at the Luixian castle for a masked ball. If we hurry, we could hold the ball before news of Violette's unfortunate mishap spreads to surrounding kingdoms?" Lord Thomise said.

"A masked ball? You want to fob me off to someone completely unseen?" Violette asked, her voice holding an edge of barely contained fury.

"No, of course not," Lord Thomise answered. "It would give suitors an opportunity to meet you. Without the—um—accident, interfering."

"Hmm... that's an interesting proposal," King Abelaird said, threading his hands on the polished table.

"Father, you can't possibly think this is a good idea? What happens when potential suitors find out about the scars? They'll think we're tricking them," Violette said, turning to King Abelaird with a pleading expression.

"The suitors won't find out. We'll make it a crime for anyone in Luixe to discuss the situation," Lord Ravelle answered.

From his crouched position under the leaf, Auber watched the council members consider the suggestion. Lord Mihaul and Lord Dukek looked unsure, but the others shared mingled glances of relief and hope. Auber snuck a peek at Violette, who sat stiff in her chair, face bearing a look of shock and outrage.

"What about the law? Don't I get to choose my suitor?" Violette asked.

"Of course, dear, you would still choose. In fact, this gives you more choices," Lord Tiernan answered smoothly.

"What do you think, darling?" King Abelaird asked.

"Fine," Violette answered, lowering her head.

"Wonderful, and remember to keep using the salve, darling. You know those salves are expensive, and I don't need to remind you how low funds are," Lord Thomise reminded Violette in a smarmy tone.

Defeated, Violette slumped lower in her seat. "I'll use the salve."

The meeting continued. Unfamiliar with Luixe politics, they lost Auber a few times, but he managed to learn that the Luixian navy desperately needed an upgrade, and the new Iasian fleet was eating further into the Luixian shipping trade. Auber tucked this information in the back of his mind. If he was staying in Luixe, he needed to keep abreast with current events. As to the identity of the treasury thief, Auber had no idea.

The council meeting finally ended, and as agreed, Violette remained seated until everyone left the chamber.

"What did you think of father's council members?" Violette asked, opening the little bag for Auber to crawl inside.

"They're certainly desperate to marry you off," Auber commented.

"Tell me about it," Violette answered, frowning. "I was hoping to delay my marriage for a few years, and this financial situation changed everything."

"You didn't want to marry?" Auber asked.

"Not really," Violette admitted. "I enjoy making my own decisions. If I marry, I'll be under someone's thumb. You've seen the way the council acts as if I'm some doll for them to use as bait. It would be worse."

"I suppose," Auber said, considered Violette's point of view. He knew she had a reputation of being independent, but he hadn't realized Violette had such a fierce streak of independence running through her veins.

"I don't think father's council ever intended to let me rule," Violette added. "They know father lets me do what I want, and they're taking advantage of this opportunity."

"Do you want to rule the Luixian kingdom?" Auber asked.

Auber's bag lurched as Violette shrugged. "The council meetings are boring, but I enjoyed seeing people when I travelled. I think if I ruled, I'd do more of that instead of hiding in the castle. Father goes to council meetings, but he hasn't attended audiences with citizens since mother passed away."

"He doesn't?" Auber wasn't aware of this development. "How long ago did your mother pass away?"

"I was so young when she passed away, so I only have a few memories of my mother. But I know Father was different then. Happier," Violette said, her voice low.

"What was she like? Queen..."

"My mother, Queen Valencia? She was stunningly beautiful, kind, and she made people happy."

Auber could understand how Queen Valencia would have been beautiful. Violette was perhaps the most exquisite woman he'd ever seen. Not that he'd seen many women locked away on Lord Ruben's estate.

Violette sighed again. "We're no closer to finding the embezzler than before, are we?" she asked.

"I'll need more time," Auber admitted, as an idea occurred to him.

"Are we near the castle garden?" he asked.

"I suppose, why?" Violette asked.

"I have a companion. I overheard some very interesting things when I was living in that pond. Maybe she could keep an ear out for useful information."

"A companion, another frog?" Violette asked, voice filled with curiosity.

"Yes, we arrived in Luixe together."

Auber felt cool air wafting by and specks of sunlight gleaming through the fabric, telling him they were entering the castle gardens. Moments later, Violette set Auber's bag by the pond.

"Therese? Therese?" Auber called. He hopped closer, peering over the surface of the water. "Therese should be around somewhere," Auber muttered. He spotted a dark green shine that was Therese basking on a lily pad. She blinked sleepily when he called her name.

"You're back." Therese closed her eyes again.

"Therese, wake up." Auber glanced around the garden, hoping no one was listening.

"Oh. Of course." Therese flicked her tongue.

"Therese, we need your help."

"Of course," Therese answered, eyes flicking back and forth over the water as she watched a water strider.

"Therese. Can you keep an ear out and listen for any suspicious conversations? We think there's a plot against King Abelaird."

"Anything suspicious, certainly," Therese agreed. She watched the water strider intently as it wandered closer.

"Therese, this is important." Auber hopped a little closer.

"Therese. If you hear anything, we'll reward you with... with..." Violette's veiled head turned toward Auber.

"With a job as the castle pastry chef," Auber blurted.

"Therese bakes?" Violette threw Auber a suspicious look.

"Therese wasn't always a frog, she's good; I promise, she makes the best ginger cake you ever ate in your life." Auber answered.

Therese sat up, some part of her amphibian brain awaked by this reminder of her past life.

"Truly?" she asked.

"I promise," Violette said in a firm voice.

CHAPTER 8

The council lost no time sending invitations for the masked ball. They invited the Luixian nobility as well as a curated selection of wealthy eligible lords from neighboring kingdoms.

A thinly disguised attempt to marry off a princess, Auber thought as he accompanied Violette to her first mask fitting; she needed one with full coverage.

A mask elegant yet fantastic enough to stand out from swarms of rich nobility and royalty,

Violette's mask was pearly white, decorated with brilliant diamonds and soft feathers. The contrast with her dark hair and blue eyes was stunning. Her dress was white to match the mask, falling in billowing folds that skimmed across her slender figure. It was modest, yet elegant, covering every inch of Violette's scars.

Violette twisted and turned, gazing critically in the mirror. "Are you sure it's secure? If the mask slips, it will be a disaster."

"It's secure, Your Highness," the artisan said, reassuring Violette by tugging the mask.

Violette pursed her lips in response. Although she applied her salves and potions religiously, they were making no visible difference. The scars were still standing in stark contrast to Violette's creamy skin.

Violette sighed, untying the slender satin ribbons that laced the mask to her face. The artisan took the mask with careful hands, placing it in a velvet box for safekeeping.

"I'll have the mask delivered after I make the adjustments," the artisan said, bowing.

"Do you have an apprentice, Grundam?" Violette asked, flicking curious eyes over the artisan's face. "It must be terribly busy with everyone needing masks."

"No, Your Highness. Who can afford apprentices these days?" he answered, then clamped his lips together with a wary expression.

"Are apprentices that expensive?" Violette asked.

"There's the apprentice tax, Your Highness; most artisans can't afford it," the artisan answered, lowering his eyes.

Violette nodded, although the line of puzzlement remained between her eyes.

"Why would father's council tax artisans for having apprentices?" Violette asked Auber as they swept down the corridor.

Auber shrugged, then realized Violette couldn't see him inside the confines of his bag. "I suppose they needed the money," he answered.

"It seems severe; the artisans were the lifeblood of the kingdom."

Auber agreed, although kept his thoughts to himself. The artisan's of Luixe produced magnificent work; it was a shame to lose it.

"I need to learn how long these artisan taxes have been levied," Violette said, continuing down the hall. Auber braved a peek outside the bag as Violette glided past her room and down the corridor, halting in front of King Abelaird's study. She rapped, not waiting for an answer before flinging the door open.

"Darling?" King Abelaird said, greeting his daughter from his plush chair by the window where he was studying a sheaf of parchments.

"Good morning, Father." Violette dropped a kiss on her father's cheek. She perched on the settee, turning the scarred side of her face away from her father. Violette set Auber's bag by her feet and Auber poked his head out, wanting to see how Violette's conversation with King Abelaird played out. Having such a strange relationship with his own father made him curious about hers.

"What brings you here?" King Abelaird shuffled his parchments, setting them on a side table. *Upside down*, Auber noted with interest. Whatever was in those papers was something King Abelaird intended to keep private from Violette.

"I was returning from the mask fitting, and I thought I'd stop by."

"Ah... the mask fitting." King Abelaird raised his glass, taking a sip. "Did you ask Grundam to make your masks?"

"He *is* the best." Violette leaned back in her seat. "It's a shame he doesn't have an apprentice; I don't know who I'll get when he retires," Violette answered, batting her lashes.

"Why this sudden interest in Grundam's apprentice?" King Abelaird said, flicking his eyes toward his daughter.

"Well... I love beautiful things, so I want to make sure someone talented replaces him," Violette answered, pouting. "It must be the apprentice tax. How long ago did we levy that one?" she asked, tapping slender fingers on the arm of her chair.

King Abelaird rubbed his chin. "Apprentice tax? About ten years ago; I suppose we could waive the tax... for Grundam if he's that important to you," the king said, casting an indulgent look at Violette.

"I suppose." Violette sighed. "I wonder how many other artisans we'll lose. I'd hate to be forced to travel to Iasia or Lovan to buy nice things. Especially, when Luixe was known as the center of fashion; our artisans are our best exporters."

"Oh darling, I hadn't thought of that," King Abelaird answered. "I suppose I could speak to the council about it. I'll add it to the agenda for the next meeting."

"Thank you, Father," Violette said, smiling. "I suppose I should leave you to your paperwork?" she glanced at the sheaf of papers at King Abelaird's elbow. "Unless you'd like help?"

"No. Nothing to worry your pretty head about," King Abelaird said, watching as Violette left the room, letting the door whisper to a close behind her.

"And that's how it's done. By the end of next council meeting, the apprentice tax will be abolished," Violette announced with satisfaction.

They'd arrived in her room, where Bane was sticking his nose under Violette's hand, begging for attention. Violette stroked him absent-mindedly.

"I have to admit. That was impressive," Auber answered. "But what happens when your father isn't around? The council won't answer to your every whim."

Violette's smile slid from her face. "I suppose I'd have to find another way," she answered slowly. Her eyes were thoughtful.

"Don't you want people to listen to you?" Auber asked. The thought of Violette being trampled over by aggressive council members didn't appeal to him; she was intelligent enough to make decisions for herself.

"I just don't know how to make the council listen to me," Violette answered with a troubled expression.

"Information." The answer came easily to Auber. The most important lesson he'd learned from Lord Ruben was that knowledge was power.

Violette sniffed. "You mean all the facts and figures in those boring council meetings?"

"No. Think about it," Auber answered. "You didn't know how the apprentice tax affected people until Grundam told you. That wasn't boring, was it?"

"I—I guess not."

"There are many ways to get knowledge. You decide how to set up your own methods. That way, when you go to the council meetings, you'll be able to speak convincingly."

"Like a personal spy network?" Violette asked, eyes sparkling with interest.

Not exactly what Auber had in mind, but a start.

"I could recruit people, everyone from servants to nobility. We could find out who's been siphoning treasury funds."

"It's the best way to find out, isn't it?" Auber asked, watching the excitement transform Violette's face.

A knock at the door interrupted them.

"I'm here to take Bane for his walk." Arel came softly into the room. She stroked Bane on the head as he waved his tail, barking when he saw the lead in her hand.

"Arel. Did you know about the apprentice tax?" Violette asked.

Arel blinked. Violette rarely sought opinions from servants.

"Um... I believe I've heard of the extra taxes, Your Highness," Arel answered in a hesitant voice. Her face betraying the fact she knew more than she was letting on.

"Oh, are there many other taxes?" Violette asked.

"I understand there are others, Your Highness," Arel answered, fastening the lead around Bane's neck.

"Hmm... I suppose we should find a list somewhere." Violette waved her hand as Arel led Bane away, a relieved expression on her face.

"I don't want father to get suspicious. I suppose I could get into his study while he's at dinner." Violette threw Auber a grin. "Are you up for some spying?"

CHAPTER 9

Auber wished he'd never introduced the idea of spying into Violette's head. She'd excused herself from dinner early, pleading a blinding headache, and now they were hovering outside King Abelaird's study.

"How will you get in?" Auber asked.

Violette slid a brass key out of her pocket with a sly grin.

"I've had a copy of father's key for ages. He gave me one when he was away on a hunting trip and never asked me to return it. I think he's forgotten I have key."

Violette slid the key into the lock and twisted it. The door opened with a soft click and she slipped inside, leaving it cracked.

"You stand guard. I'm going to find the tax papers. We should be safe for at least half an hour," Violette said, heading for the wide desk where she began rifling through papers and poking through ledgers.

"These numbers are confusing," Violette complained, studying a row of figures.

"Well, the tax laws probably won't be written in a nice tidy list for you," Auber said. "You'll have to piece the information together."

Violette groaned. "I don't have time to read these papers now. I'll take some with me, older ones he might not miss and read the current ones here," Violette said, flipping through another ledger before stuffing it into a large satchel.

Half an hour was not enough time. Auber grew tense as the minutes ticked by, and Violette was no closer to discovering anything of value.

"How much time do we have left?" Violette blew a strand of dark hair from her eyes.

"Five minutes." Auber sucked in a sharp breath as he heard movement down the corridor, then relaxed as the footsteps passed.

Violette grabbed a few more papers. "Wait, I've found something, an expense sheet." She clutched a parchment, a triumphant smile spreading across her face. "And here's another." She stuffed them between the ledgers before rising to her feet. "I'll have to hope Father doesn't look for these before I can return them." Violette whisked the papers into neat piles. "There, I'm ready."

She strolled across the carpet, bag swinging from her hand.

"Someone's coming," Auber whispered.

"Now?" Panic flared in Violette's eyes.

"Yes. They're headed this way. Hide." Auber hopped behind a flowing drape.

Violette frantically scanned the room, scampering behind the settee just as the door opened.

Auber crouched low, peeking around the velvet, as King Abelaird entered the chamber followed by Lord Sidelle. Lord Sidelle took a place on the settee, stretching crossed legs in front of him. King Abelaird went to the cabinet.

"Care for a drink?" the king lifted a crystal decanter.

"Yes, please."

King Abelaird poured two fingers of liquid in each glass, swirling them before handing one to Lord Sidelle.

"Ah," Lord Sidelle said, sipping from his glass. "Nice to get away from the constant prattle at those castle dinners. I don't know how you put up with it."

King Abelaird pursed his lips. "It's not so terrible when you get used to it."

Lord Sidelle shook his head, dark hair flopping over his forehead. "If you'd remarried, things would be easier. Someone to share the burden."

"Or create more burden," King Abelaird answered with a wry twist of his lips.

Lord Sidelle remained silent, realizing he was veering into sensitive territory. King Abelaird rarely talked about his widowed status; and never in front of Violette.

"I've brought you here for a reason," King Abelaird broke the silence. "I think you know what it is."

"The cure," Lord Sidelle answered.

King Abelaird nodded. The only betrayal of his feelings, the slight tremble of his hand clutching the glass.

Out of the corner of his eye, Auber saw Violette's foot twitch from her place behind the settee. This must be the cure for Violette's scar. *I wonder if Violette knew he'd sent the council members on the search for a cure,* Auber wondered, his eyes fixed on Lord Sidelle.

"I've scoured the healing guild, sent men into every nook and cranny of Luixe and beyond." Lord Sidelle shook his head.

"Nothing?" King Abelaird asked.

"Nothing you haven't already tried."

"I worry Violette's not ready. The council could help her, but it's clear I can't trust everyone," King Abelaird said, staring at the glass in his hand.

"Give it time," Lord Sidelle answered. "Don't lose hope; we've heard great things about the healers in Iasia and Lovan. Perhaps we'll discover a cure yet."

"But when? We don't have time. I'd hoped for Violette to marry someone independent, so she would have recourse when I'm gone. Someone on her side without internal ties."

Auber's thoughts screeched to a halt.

When I'm gone. The words rang like bells.

Auber stared at King Abelaird, his mouth hanging open.

This isn't about Violette. This is about King Abelaird.

Auber studied King Abelaird. He looked healthy. He acted healthy. What could possibly be wrong with him? The illness or malady must be serious, even fatal, if King Abelaird was concerned enough to ensure Violette would be cared for in his impeding absence.

"I'll keep searching," Lord Sidelle said, snatching a worried glance at the king. He threw back the last dregs of his drink before taking his leave.

After Lord Sidelle's retreat, the king sat on. So long that Auber was afraid King Abelaird would fall asleep. Finally, he set down his glass and retreated, locking the door carefully behind him.

Violette stood, rubbing the circulation back into her legs.

"I thought they would never leave," she said, her voice unnaturally bright, her eyes shiny.

"Violette?" Auber's voice was soft. "Violette, did you know?"

"Know what?" Violette's voice cracked. She fumbled for the key, sliding it into the lock.

"Did you know your father... King Abelaird was ill?"

"Um. No?" Violette whispered. "Why would he tell Lord Sidelle and not me? I'm his daughter." She wiped her cheek.

"King Abelaird wants to protect you," Auber answered. "Anyone can see that."

"Well, it's not working very well, is it?" Violette sniffed. She grated the key in the lock. "What else is he hiding from me?" she snatched up the bag; Auber had to scramble before falling on the floor.

"Violette, your father loves you. Very much. At least you have that." The cloth bag muffled Auber's voice.

At least she has a father that cares, Auber thought. His own father had only wanted him to be useful. He glared at his frog legs.

"I suppose." Violette arrived at her own chambers. "But I wish father would have trusted me."

"Violette, love is free. You have to earn trust," Auber's voice was gentle.

Violette huffed, setting the bag into the armoire so Auber could climb out.

"I suppose you're right. But how am I supposed to earn father's trust now? It's too late." She frowned in the mirror and picked up one of her salves. The chamber filled with the smell of clove, comfrey, and calunda. Violette dabbed some salve on her scar with her pinkie finger.

"How?" she capped the salve.

"Take an interest," Auber answered. "The taxes were a start. King Abelaird wants to know you can handle ruling the kingdom. That you'll survive. Thrive."

"But what if I don't thrive?" Violette asked in a tiny voice. She sat at the vanity and put her head in her hands.

"You will thrive," Auber insisted. "I've seen you. You are formidable. Find your way to do it."

Violette tied a smock around her waist and headed for her painting.

"I suppose." Her eyes were thoughtful. "You know... you're not too bad for a frog."

Auber felt a warmth kindle deep inside.

And that wasn't all Auber felt. He felt a strange stretching sensation, tugging his skin and body. He looked down, curious about the tingling sensation that swarmed across his body. His skin looked the same. But wait? Was it a shade or two lighter? Less green? Auber gave himself a critical look. It was too hard to tell in this dim light. He would have to check again during daylight.

"I suppose I should read those papers we borrowed from Father's study." Violette was completely unaware of the strange sensations Auber was experiencing. "Can frogs read? I could use help."

CHAPTER 10

"There's nothing useful in these documents," Violette said, rubbing her temple.

"Keep looking, you'll find a clue somewhere." Auber flipped another page over. He'd discovered a clever way to turn pages with webbed feet and was quite proud of himself. He was a little taller too—the tugging sensation must have grown him.

Violette studied a row of figures in a thick ledger. "This is just another expense statement. Animal feed, shipping fees, imports; that sort of thing."

"Shipping fees, for imports or exports?"

"I don't know." Violette huffed. "Does it matter?"

"Of course it matters. If you're shipping exports, it means Luixe is producing something. Something valuable to other kingdoms."

"Oh." Violette flipped through the pages. "This appears to be exports."

"Very good." Auber hopped over to the pages. "What does Luixe produce and export?"

Violette shrugged. "We barely sustain enough agriculture to grow enough food for ourselves. So not that. We've little timber, no mines, the artisans are disappearing at an alarming rate."

"But where does the Luixe economy excel?" Auber asked.

"We have beautiful landscapes, fast horses. We used to have wine from vineyards. I'm not sure what happened to them... fires?" Violette said with a shudder, remembering her own painful encounter with the flames.

"That's it, the vineyards. How could I have forgotten?" Auber said, bouncing in excitement.

"What exactly happened to the vineyards?" he pressed.

"The vineyards were located in southern Luixe. Of course, the crown owns vineyards, but Lord Tiernan and Lord Dukek managed them because their estates are down South. There was a drought. The vineyards were bone-dry and fires swept through, destroying everything. It was years ago, but according to father, the vineyards never grew back. That's when the tide turned."

"And King Abelaird trusts Lord Tiernan and Lord Dukek?" Auber asked.

"Implicitly," Violette said, her voice strong and sure.

Auber glanced at the list of figures again. "If this is correct, it seems you're still exporting a substantial amount of product. We must learn what that product is, and where the money's disappearing to."

"Wouldn't father notice if Luixe was exporting and not getting paid for it?" Violette asked, troubled eyes staring at the rows of figures.

"Not if King Abelaird wasn't well; not if he was distracted."

"I wish father would confide in me."

"Likely, King Abelaird didn't want to worry you," Auber answered, hating the sadness lurking in Violette's eyes and wishing he could alleviate her pain.

Violette flipped over another page, sighing as she studied the numbers.

The next morning, Violette woke early, slipping into King Abelaird's study to return the documents. This time, without incident, she reported back to Auber.

The day of masked ball drew increasingly near. Every day, guests trickled into the Luixian castle at a steady rate. Auber wondered privately how the castle afforded to wine and dine the noble guests. Even the prince of Iasia attended, much to King Abelaird and the council's delight.

King Abelaird and the council invited Prince Landry to dine at the royal table at every possible opportunity. Aubrey had to admit, the young prince was an ideal match for Violette— handsome, clever, affable, and extremely rich. Not only did Prince Landry have access to the wealthy Iasian crown, his family was affluent in their own right, with healthy estates spread across various parts of Iasia.

"How do you feel about Prince Landry?" Auber asked, crouching by the window and admiring the sunset over castle gardens.

"Landry is... pleasant." Violette said, shrugging. Auber couldn't read Violette's facial expression behind the thick veil.

"Pleasant? Just Pleasant?" Aubrey asked.

"Yes, pleasant.... Nice, " Violette replied, staring across the rippling water. "I wanted to have a marriage like father and mother. By all accounts, they were madly in love. I look at Prince Landry and feel... nice.... Good at best. I want more. Besides, under these circumstances, it's not like we can become properly acquainted. Father makes me sit behind the screen and watch during dinner parties, and goodness knows what Landry thinks."

Aubrey nodded. Because of the council's determination to keep Violette's unsightly scars private, she sat hidden behind a screen at the dinner table. King Abelaird had announced she was away at the summer castle. Auber felt sorry for princess Violette, sneaking in before dinner and slipping out after the last guest departed. It must be humiliating beyond measure. Violette showed no sign of distress at the uncomfortable situation, but it rankled Auber deep in his core. Although, he would ever mention this to Violette, she suffered enough.

"Maybe you'll feel sparks when you meet Prince Landry at the masked ball." The words slipped out before Auber could pull them back. He was torn. Auber wanted Violette's happiness. He did. However, the terror of being trapped in a frog body for the rest of his life was quickly being overshadowed by the thought of seeing his new companion on someone else's arm and brought an edge of misery to his soul. Feelings Auber didn't realize he was capable of.

"That reminds me, my ball gown arrived. If Arel laces the gown for me, will you give me an unbiased opinion?" Violette asked, tossing Auber a wheedling smile.

"I suppose, although why you'd ask my opinion is a mystery. I'm hardly an expert on fancy ballgowns," Auber said.

"That's why I asked you." Violette laughed. "Arel will be here in a moment. I asked her to come early." She sat at the vanity, moving her pots of cream around. "Did you see the gold and blue salve pot?" she asked Auber, a wrinkle between her eyes.

"No, maybe Arel moved it," Auber replied, still distracted by the thought of Auber and Prince Landry together.

Just then, Arel arrived. Violette and Arel disappeared into the dressing room while Auber waited, nibbling on a lettuce leaf and wondering if he should visit Therese at the pond that evening.

Violette emerged, twirling in her flowing white gown. Auber swallowed the lettuce leaf, choking as it caught in his throat.

Violette was beautiful.

Auber always knew Violette was beautiful.

But this was different.

This was a beauty that pulled at his core, tugging out feelings he didn't realize existed.

Violette preened and fluffed in front of the mirror. "What do you think?"

"Nice," Auber squeaked.

He felt a painful throbbing stretching his webbed feet.

Auber looked down. What was happening? His feet were changing, narrowing, the webbing shrinking and growing thin. He wriggled his toes cautiously as the pain diminished.

"Is something wrong?" Violette heard Auber's startled cry.

"Everything's fine," Auber answered, his voice high and squeaky.

Violette shot Auber a suspicious look but remained silent.

Auber examined his toes again. Hi feet appeared less... froglike. For the first time, a ray of hope darted through his chest. Ruben's spell was weakening.

CHAPTER 11

Preparations for the masked ball intensified into a frenzy.

As the council and King Abelaird promised, Luixian citizens weren't allowed to breathe a word of Violette's condition. Anyone caught doing so was under threat of either having their estates removed from them or being confined to the dungeon. Violette stayed hidden from the foreign guests, remaining heavily veiled whenever she ventured into the public areas of the castle; King Abelaird's council strictly banned visitors from visiting royal apartments.

"I can't wait until this palaver is over," Violette said, adjusting her veil with a heavy sigh. "This is getting ridiculous and I'm dying for fresh air; let's walk in the garden."

She held out the bag for Auber to hop inside. It was a struggle, Auber needed to squeeze into the bag.

"Violette, is this the same bag you always use?" Auber wriggled, trying to get comfortable.

"Yes, why?" Violette lifted the bag and slung it over her shoulder.

"It feels tight."

"Too much rich castle foods," Violette said, fastening a collar and leash around Bane's neck.

Auber sniffed. His skin had felt tight since yesterday, like it was growing too small for his body.

"Will you focus, Auber?" Violette said in a scolding tone as she lifted the bag. "The masked ball is tomorrow. I'll need help."

"Of course," Auber answered, dragging his attention away from his changing body. "What do you need? You know I'm not great with gowns, shoes, or jewelry."

Violette snorted. "I have a dresser for that. I need you to spy at the ball and learn about the different candidates."

Auber swallowed hard at this reminder that Violette's purpose was to find a suitable match. He'd sat beside her, peeking through her screen at dinner to inspect all new arrivals, but the ball made everything real. Too real.

"Of course," Auber agreed. "Anything in particular we're looking for?"

"Father and the council care most about how rich the candidates are. But I'll let the council conduct their own investigations. I need to know the important things; I'm going to live and rule beside this person. If only we could listen to the servants' gossip because servants have the best opportunity to observe the candidates unnoticed."

"You want me to go the servants' wing before and listen to their conversations? Is there any candidate in particular you have your eye on?"

Violette pursed her lips thoughtfully. "That Iasian prince seems an excellent candidate. Father said the family mines and the Luixian artisans need the resources."

"You want me to investigate Prince Landry of Iasia?" Auber asked, his heart sinking.

Violette's eyes lit up. "Could you? I was watching him at dinner last night and he so handsome."

Auber popped his head out of the bag. "I suppose, but how am I supposed to get to the servant's wing?"

Violette tapped her chin with a slender finger.

"I have an idea," she said, picking up Auber's bag and heading back to her chambers.

Hours later, Auber was crouched inside a silver dome on a plate of discarded sandwiches. Violette's plan was to order food, then send Auber on the plate back to the castle kitchens. Auber moved his foot, wiping off a scrap of salmon and a limp shred of lettuce.

"There you are; took long enough," someone scolded the serving maid as she set the domed platter down with a thunk. Auber's stomach rolled as the tray swung through the air. "It's so busy with Princess's guests here. Like the staff don't have extra work piling up already with the wages lowered and staff cut in a single week. We're not miracle workers here."

Auber's ears pricked. Had the council cut the staff and the wages? He wondered if Violette and King Abelaird were privy to this knowledge. He doubted it. Auber tucked the snippet of information away and continued listening.

"Should we wash these dishes now or wait for the rest of the trays to arrive?"

"Wash them now," the voice said.

Auber's heart lurched. He hadn't planned on being discovered so soon. A careless oversight, he realized as plates clattered less than a foot away. Auber held his breath, wondering if he could slip out and dash away now.

A split second later, a burst of light assaulted his eyes, and a piercing shriek ripped through the air.

"Nasty, horrible creature! What is that?"

Auber didn't wait to hear more. He leapt to the floor and galloped frantically for the door, which fortunately was left open.

"Don't stand there. Catch it. If a frog gets into the guest room, we'll pay for it."

Auber's feet scrabbled against the rough flagstones, grappling for purchase. Eyes fixed on the door, he jumped through, narrowly missing a wooden broomstick swinging through the air. The corridor was empty, with few places to hide. Auber cursed Violette's optimism in concocting this hare-brained plan as he skittered across the floor, heading for a sideboard lined with fine china dishes. If he could squeeze under the sideboard, the kitchen maids couldn't reach him. Breathing hard, Auber dived into the blessed darkness.

"Get him with the broom handle," shrieked the voice.

Auber's heart thudded against his chest as the wooden broom handle prodded under the sideboard. He couldn't stay here. He had to escape down the corridor to find safety.

The broom handle swung again, nearly whacking Auber on the head. He peered out from under the sideboard, noticing halfway down the corridor the laundry door stood open. If he could reach that doorway, perhaps he could find a better hiding place. Auber took a deep breath and ran.

Auber's sturdy legs pumped wildly as he flew through the air, two angry and surprised kitchen maids in hot pursuit. He careened around the corner into the laundry room.

Piles of clothes littered the floor, with tubs and wooden buckets lining the wall. A treasure trove of hiding places.

Auber scooted under a pile of linens as the kitchen maids tore around the corner.

"Where is that creature?" the kitchen maid screeched, her hair wild around her red face.

"What creature?" the laundress asked, turning with a disapproving frown. Kitchen maids weren't welcome in the laundry.

Auber shrank under the linen sheet. No one had seen him come in. He was safe for now. He caught his breath.

"A nasty, slimy frog. It hopped in here."

"There's no frog in our laundry," the laundress said, huffing.

"I saw it," the kitchen maid insisted.

"Well, you're welcome to search. Just don't dirty the clothes or linens," the laundress said, returning to her soapy bucket.

Several minutes passed. Tense minutes.

Auber huddled deeper into his hiding place, scooting further and further back as several laundresses joined the kitchen maids to search for the wayward amphibian. They came close, nearly discovering him when they lifted the bedclothes wadded next to him. Fortunately, Auber was far enough back to remain undetected.

"You must have imagined it because there are no frogs here." The head laundress flicked her fingers, shooing the kitchen maids back to their own territory.

"If he shows up in some fine lady's chemise, it's your responsibility," the kitchen maid warned as she retreated.

The laundress snorted, returning to her duties.

Auber relaxed. The laundry room was warm and comfortable. He settled into his hiding place, tuning into the gossip.

"Mary, did you see what Lady Temperly was wearing yesterday?" a laundress asked, swishing the clothes in a bucket.

"Trying to catch Duke of Issa's eye." Mary snorted. "She's better off looking elsewhere. Watch what you 're doing with that silk. Remember, cold water only, Hannah."

Auber's ears pricked. Lord Issa was one of the prime contenders for Violette's crown.

"Why shouldn't Lady Temperly be interested in the duke. He's handsome. And obscenely rich," Hannah replied.

Water splashed and trickled— someone wringing wet clothes.

"Yes. But Lord Issa's not picky enough, if you catch my drift," Mary said. "The Duke of Issa can't keep his hands off any lady. You know yourself the trouble the serving girls have avoiding his unwanted advances."

Hannah sighed. "I suppose. Shame, the money would be nice."

Auber sighed. He supposed the Duke of Issa would cut be off Violette's list now. He had a feeling Violette didn't fancy sharing her future partner.

"And what about Lord Bryan? He's newly widowed. He's inherited his wife's estate as well as his mother's. Lady Bryan was an only child, poor thing," Hannah continued. Auber heard wet fabric rubbing against the washboard in a sudsy rhythm.

"Didn't you hear why Lady Bryan passed?" Mary said, lowering her voice to a whisper.

Auber strained to listen.

"Why?" Hannah said, tone dripping with anticipation.

"The elder Lord Bryan killed her."

"Lord Bryan murdered her?" Hannah squeaked. "How do you know?"

"Well," Mary answered, pausing for maximum effect. "I know because my cousin John worked in the Bryan's estate. In the stable."

Hannah remained silent.

"The stable," Mary repeated. "The stable where Lady Bryan kept her horse. The horse that killed her."

"Oh," Hannah said. "That's right, Lady Bryan died of a head injury."

"Well. John told my Simeon, my brother, and Simeon told me. John found muckweed seeds in the horse feed. But only the feed given to Lady Bryan's pony. That pony was well mannered and gentle, according to John. A perfect record. Never would have hurt a fly."

Hannah gasped in mingled shock and delight.

"That's not all," Mary continued, enjoying the attention. "John accompanied Lady Bryan when she rode. He said Lady Bryan often had bruises. And once came out with a limp. Said she fell down the stairs."

"Do you think the elder Lord Bryan pushed the Lady Bryan?" Hannah whispered.

"Or worse," Mary answered.

Auber heard a laundry basket scrape across the floor as the girls pushed the clothes to the courtyard to hang. He peeped from behind his hiding place, noticing his side of the laundry room was empty. Keeping close to the wall, Auber crept around the edge of the room, keeping a close eye on where the other laundresses stood stirring boiling white linens in giant copper kettles over a roaring fire.

He slipped into the courtyard; there were plenty of hiding places. Hannah and Mary chattered, oblivious to Auber's presence as they pegged clothes on the clotheslines. They were so involved in their conversation, they didn't notice him hopping through the overgrown grass. Auber eyed the half-open door across the courtyard, deciding that would be his next destination.

Auber slipped unnoticed into a long, dark corridor. The servants' wing. Most servants were working, and the corridor lay still in echoing silence. Auber made his way down the dim, silent corridor, climbing several flights of stairs. He'd paid close attention to directions as Violette had lugged his bag around the castle.

He wandered until he eventually found himself in familiar territory, only once forced to hide under a table as a group of court noblewomen passed, giggling and gossiping as they pranced down the corridor.

Presently, Auber entered a spacious salon. He glanced around, thinking the salon was the kind of room Violette must have frequented before the accident scarred her. Quiet luxury emanated from every corner of the elegantly appointed room. Auber's feet sunk into plush soft carpet, and a table laden with delicate refreshments stood in the center of the room; a silver teapot steamed gently and filled the room with its fragrant aroma.

Auber wriggled under a low settee and crouched near the wall, assuming if hot tea was waiting, people would arrive soon.

Not a moment too soon, the bevy of giggling girls swept into the salon in a flurry of silk skirts, jewels, and expensive perfume. A maid scurried in after them and began pouring tea.

"I can't wait until the masked ball." One of the girls perched on the settee Auber was hiding under. "I have the most gorgeous, marvelous mask. Gold and blue to match my eyes and hair."

Auber glanced over. Bejewelled velvet slippers rested gracefully on the floor a foot away from him.

"My mask is red and silver," another girl joined her, and the dainty settee creaked under their combined weight.

"I wonder what Violette will wear," another wondered with an accompanying titter.

The girl in the bejewelled slippers huffed. "Knowing Violette, she'll show off."

"Well, it is Violette's ball, Lady Sophie," the other girl answered.

The girl with the red mask, I'll look for her at the ball. Violette needs to know who she can trust, Auber thought.

"Violette always has to one up everyone," Sophie continued. "It's not like people won't find out she's damaged, eventually."

"Hush. We aren't allowed to say anything about Violette's accident," a girl scolded.

Auber peeked from under the settee, watching two girls take chairs across from him. They must be Luixian noblewomen if they knew about Violette's accident and were discussing it freely.

Sophie sniffed. "Who does King Abelaird's council think they're fooling? I mean, Violette's already crown princess; anyone would marry her for the throne. Who cares if she's not pretty anymore?"

Anger surged through Auber's veins. How dare these prissy noble girls insinuate his Violette was ugly? For one brief second, Auber considered hurling himself at the girl, imagining the look of surprise as hot tea spilled down that delicate silk dress. But Auber restrained himself, instead keeping his ears tuned for more titbits.

"I heard the council spent a fortune on the masked ball," Lady Sophie continued. "I can't wait to see it."

Auber wondered how King Abelaird afforded the expense of the ball. A loan from council members, perhaps? Unfortunately, the conversation wandered into other territory and Auber soon bored of tedious discussions of dresses and jewels and longed for the girls to leave. Eventually, they trickled out; no doubt to prepare themselves for another of the castle's formal dinners. Violette wasn't the only person attempting to snare a wealthy, noble husband.

Auber waited until the kitchen maid cleared away the tea tray before crawling from under the settee, stretching his cramping legs in relief. He'd been growing so fast, it wasn't easy to fit under furniture anymore. He wandered the corridors until he found the royal wing.

CHAPTER 12

Auber shifted inside his makeshift armoire home. Violette's chambers were a hotbed of frantic preparation for the masked ball. The air was thick with scented perfumes and oils. Violette's luxurious dark hair was being combed into a complicated pile of curls. The treasury had been raided for the most expensive and ostentatious crown jewels. Jewels that would mark Violette as princess and heir despite her masked state.

At least Violette was ready. She couldn't carry Auber in her tiny jewelled reticule, so after some discussion, Violette arranged for Arel to deliver Auber to her private powder room adjoining the ballroom in a leather case, one that ostensibly held cosmetics. From there, Violette could sneak him into the ballroom under her wrap.

A knock sounded at the door, and Arel hurried to answer it.

"Father?" Violette said, questions in her voice.

King Abelaird slipped inside the chambers. "Darling, may I speak with you for a moment? In private, please."

The handmaids took King Abelaird's cue, moving into the corridor and leaving King Abelaird alone with his daughter.

"Yes, Father?" Violette said, standing straight and tall, gloved hands folded in front of her.

"You studied the list my council provided you?" King Abelaird asked.

"Yes, Father."

The council had tasked Violette with memorizing the most wealthy eligible bachelors. Unfortunately, Lord Bryan was near the top of the list. Violette would have a fine line to walk in order to keep King Abelaird's council members content.

"Prince Landry should be your primary target. I've been told his mask is a lion. Make sure you dance with him first. Prince Landry will be directed to you, so don't approach him first."

Violette nodded obediently, white feathers on her mask bobbing.

"We'll be nearby if you require assistance." King Abelaird patted Violette on the shoulder.

"You can count on me, Father," Violette said.

King Abelaird nodded, giving his daughter one last searching look before leaving the chamber.

Violette studied her reflection in the mirror. She was perfect. The mask fitted smoothly over her features, leaving long-lashed eyes peeking out like living jewels. Violette's hair was thick and glossy, and the dress highlighted her slender curves to perfection.

In a flurry of silk and velvet, she glided away, ready for the performance of her life.

Auber squished himself into the leather case Violette had set in his armoire. It was a tight fit. He was growing faster and his features softening; his limbs shorter, his feet less webbed. Auber examined himself daily, looking for signs of the curse being lifted. His keen eyes noted that slowly and steadily, Lord Ruben's enchantment was fading.

Arel arrived and lifted the case, protesting at the weight of it. She lugged it out of the chamber, then paused, setting it down with a thump.

What is happening, Auber shifted in his dark, cramped prison.

"Silly girl, she's forgotten her combs. I'll have to bring them for her."

Before Auber knew what was happening, Arel was fumbling with the clasps. He gulped as they opened. Light flooded in, burning his eyes with brightness.

"Why are you in Violette's cosmetic case?" Arel asked, looking ready to either shriek or bolt.

"Violette put me here. We're friends; I'm helping her at the ball," Auber said, suddenly realizing "I'm keeping an eye on people for her."

"Oh," Arel said, eyes brightening. "Like you tell her what people are saying about her?"

"Yes."

"Interesting," Arel said, pursing her lips. "I've often wanted to tell Violette things people say myself. But I can't because I'm a here chambermaid."

"Like what things?" Auber perked up. Arel had access to the royal wing, the guest wing, and the servant's wing; she could be a valuable asset.

Arel paused. "Well. I think someone's stealing from Violette's chamber."

Auber's head jerked up. This fit in with Violette's conversation with King Abelaird. The treasury thief must have stolen from Violette's chambers as well.

Arel nodded. "Recently, things have gone missing. I was afraid to tell Violette, in case she blamed me."

"What items went missing?"

"Small but valuable items, like jewelry and cosmetics. But always the one's she hasn't worn in a while. Whoever the thief is, knows to take the things that won't be missed."

"So someone with access to the chambers who understands Violette's interests?"

Arel nodded.

This was an unexpected development. However, Auber could understand how Violette's stolen jewelry could remain unnoticed. The princess's dressing chamber was stuffed with jewels and clothes the princess rarely wore. It would be easy to think an item was misplaced.

"Do you have any idea who the culprit is?" Auber asked Arel.

Arel shook her head. "Few have access to the royal wing. Just the council and King Abelaird's most trusted servants."

"We'll have to watch Violette's chambers. See who comes and goes when something gets taken. Has anything disappeared recently?"

Arel pursed her lips. "It's difficult because Violette tries things on and misplaces them. But she hasn't been as keen on wardrobe changes since..."

"Since the accident?" Auber asked.

Arel bit her lip. "She's lost interest."

A pang of sadness shot through Auber as he realized the extent of Violette's loss. He vowed he would do whatever he could to help catch the thief. Starting with the masked ball. He settled deep into the case.

"Let's get to the ball."

Arel closed the lid and hefted the case, depositing it into a side room that had been designated for Violette's use during the masked ball.

It was dark and stuffy in the case. Strains of music filtered through, muffled by the walls of leather. Auber's legs were cramping from the uncomfortable position. Cramping... or was something else happening. Auber couldn't see in the pitch black interior.

Finally, footsteps entered the room. Hands fumbled with the latch, and Auber blinked against the glaring light.

Violette's sparkling eyes peered through the jewelled mask. "You made it."

Auber heard the smile in Violette's voice. "I take it the ball's a success?" he asked.

Violette smoothed her silk skirt. "I've danced with Prince Landry three times. And he left Sophie to speak to me."

A twang of jealousy pierced Auber's heart as he silently scolded himself. He wanted Violette to be happy. But how could she break the curse if she with with Prince Landry? Auber pushed away his conflicted feelings; he'd deal with them later. Besides, his head was pounding, and his skin felt itchy and tingly all over.

"Auber, are you all right?" Violette asked, peering at him with narrowed eyes.

"Of course," Auber squeaked.

"What happened to you? You look different."

Auber glanced down, then gasped. He was less froglike than ever. In fact, he looked halfway human.

"When did that happen?" Violette pointed to Auber's legs with a curious expression on her face. They were human legs. He held up his hands. Human hands. It was a pity about the size because he still fit inside the vanity case, but progress was progress.

"Are you a pixie?" Violette asked, suspicion in her voice. Pixies were rare and known for their mischievous ways.

"No," Auber answered. "I'm... cursed." He looked at his hands again, counting his fingers in wonder. "What about my face, does it look human?" Auber asked.

"Sort of," Violette answered, perching on the settee. "It's definitely changed, and it's less green. What happened to you anyways, curses aren't allowed in Luixe; whoever did that took a big risk." A hint of sympathy shone through her curiosity.

"It was my father, he liked to experiment with magic, and I guess I was a handy target." Auber answered.

"Your *father*, what kind of a father does that to their own child, can't he change you back?" Violette's eyes filled with horror.

Auber clenched his newfound hands into tiny fists. "I guess he might have, he spent a lot of money educating me. But he was in an accident before he hand the chance."

"Isn't there anything you can do about it?" Violette walked over to her easel, picking up her paint palette and setting it down again.

"I'm figuring it out." Auber said shortly, cutting her off knowing he couldn't explain how the curse would be broken without risking her finding out too much about his circumstances. That could ruin everything.

Auber cast his thoughts back. He'd felt the change when he'd first decided to help Violette. That connection must be lifting the curse. If only he could break the rest of it. Auber flexed his green tinged fingers.

"Fine, you can keep your secrets, but we'll have to decide what to do with you," Violette continued. "You can't stay in my chamber as a human. It would be inappropriate; if the council discovered you, it would be a tremendous scandal. I'll have to tell someone, I suppose."

"Can we tell Arel?" Auber suggested.

"Arel?" a thoughtful expression passed through Violette's eyes. "That could work, but is Arel loyal."

"I think so. Arel actually found me before she brought me here, and we talked," Auber admitted. He explained to Violette how Arel happened upon him while carrying the case.

"Arel will get you a bed to sleep in. There's an empty chamber in our wing you can use. Father would never notice if you kept out of his way."

Auber nodded. He'd miss Violette's cozy armoire guestroom, but she had a point. Violette couldn't afford to have him discovered in her private chambers.

"You'll need clothes too."

Auber's greenish ears tinged pink. He'd forgotten he wasn't wearing clothes.

Violette laughed, a clear tinkling sound.

"Don't worry. Arel will find you somewhere. I've got to return to the ball. They'll start whispering if I'm away too long. Besides, I need to make sure Sophie doesn't steal Prince Landry away when I'm not paying attention. I'll leave this door cracked so you can sneak out. There's a curtain drawn in front of it, and everyone knows this room is designated for me; they won't dare come inside."

Violette skipped away, buoyed by the prospect of more flirting and dancing. Auber waited until Violette was gone before walking to the door. Walking, not hopping, he reminded himself with a grin. His muscles were tired and clumsy after the change, but he managed. Auber inched the curtain back, peering out.

The ballroom was filled with color, swirling in all directions. Chandeliers scattered prisms of light across the polished marble, and lively strains of music floated through the air, mingling with the sounds of chatter and laughter as couples whirled by in a graceful dance.

Auber soaked in his first ball with wide eyes; Lord Ruben's estate never held events. He'd only seen things like this in paintings. Auber's keen eyes picked out the details. It was difficult to recognize anyone with the masks, but across the room, he saw Violette giggling with a tall figure. Prince Landry, Auber guessed.

Auber spotted out a figure in a blue and gold mask speaking to a girl in a magnificent red mask and matching silk gown. The girls from the salon, Sophie and Anna. He watched them carefully, until they moved away, obscured by dancers. The next time he spotted them, Sophie, in the blue and gold, had disappeared. Auber scanned the ballroom, but she was nowhere to be seen.

Auber shrugged off Sophie's disappearance. It was hard to keep track of anyone in this crowd. He turned his attention to King Abelaird, who was leaning over, speaking to Lord Basile. King Abelaird lifted a drink to his lips, taking a sip before continuing the conversation. A whisper of the curtains and a brush of cold air distracted Auber. He spun but saw nothing.

Disquieted, Auber turned back to Violette's room. He froze. There was a slender figure moving inside. A figure that did not belong to Violette or Arel. Auber flattened himself against the wall, peeking around the corner. Sophie, he recognized the mask and dress. She hummed, flicking through Violette's toiletries arranged on the table. Lifting a hairbrush, Sophie tapped it against her hand before digging through Auber's case.

Auber narrowed his eyes. How had Sophie gotten in Violette's room unseen? He was certain he would have noticed. Sophie stood and smoothed her hands down her blue silk gown. Then, tossing her hair, she left the room. Auber drew back into the folds of the curtain as she swished past him.

Then she was gone.

One second, she was there.

The next she wasn't.

Auber blinked, hardly daring to believe his eyes.

Was Sophie the mysterious thief, and if so, how had she gained access to Violette's chambers in the royal wing?

Sophie slipped into the crowd. Auber watched the glinting gold of her mask wink under the lights as she melted into the party goers.

The ball was magnificent, ending in a very showy, very expensive fireworks display. Auber missed the fireworks display because he'd returned to his case, now with a tight squeeze indeed, and Arel had returned him to Violette's chambers.

"I'll move you to the spare room tomorrow," Arel explained. "You'll be fine here for one more night, King Abelaird will never suspect." She brought Auber a cup of fresh, cold water. A cup! Auber was delighted to drink out of a cup.

"Have you ever noticed anything strange about Lady Sophie?" Auber asked, setting the cup down. He took one of the sandwiches Arel had brought from Violette's waiting room.

Arel tilted her head. "Lady Sophie? She's never gotten along with Violette, probably jealous. Why?"

"I thought I saw Sophie disappear." Auber knew well invisibility was a mage gift, but he'd never seen anyone use the ability before. Auber shuddered. After his own unpleasant magical experience, Auber found magic more than a little distasteful.

"I didn't know Sophie's family was gifted. Now that you mention it, she has a startling habit of popping up out of nowhere," Arel said, narrowing her eyes. Her expression of displeasure made her opinion of Sophie clear.

"And Sophie wears slippers," Auber noted.

"Slippers?"

"Soft slippers. I saw them when she went to the salon with the courtier girls. The slippers were jewelled, but they were definitely slippers with soft bottoms."

"Ah… so she can sneak around more easily; I knew Lady Sophie was trouble. She's horrible to her staff too. Someone always has to stay awake in her dressing chamber with a light because she's afraid of the dark. And she makes her servants taste her food in case there's egg in it," Arel wrinkled her nose.

"What do you think Sophie wants? Should we tell Violette we suspect she's stealing?"

"I don't know what Lady Sophie is trying to accomplish—either its making life inconvenient for Violette or she wants Prince Landry. But we should definitely inform Violette; Sophie means trouble and Violette might have more information."

"Hello, what are you two whispering about?" Violette danced inside, twirling her skirts.

Auber and Arel whipped their heads around.

Violette sat at her dressing table and fluffed her hair. "What a fantastic party; we haven't held a masked ball that good in ages." She untied the silk ribbons fastening her mask to her head.

"You enjoyed yourself, Your Highness?" Arel asked, whisking over and beginning to take the pins from Violette's dark locks.

"Oh yes. And I found Prince Landry simply divine. Sophie was spitting nails—she must have had her eye on him." Violette's hair cascaded down her back. "Not that it matters," she added quickly.

"Speaking of Sophie," Arel hesitated. "Have you ever noticed anything strange about her?"

The wrinkle appeared between Violette's eyes. "Strange, what kind of strange?"

"I saw Sophie disappear," Auber interrupted.

Violette turned. "She can do that?"

"I think so." Auber added, "Sophie came sneaking into the side room. I was behind the curtain and heard it move but never saw anything. Then she appeared in your room. Out of thin air."

Violette's eyes widened. "There were whispers that Sophie's family was gifted. But they've never displayed it, not in court."

"Her family? Who else is in Lady Sophie's family?" Auber questioned.

"Her mother, she resides at the country estate—doesn't enjoy socialising. And Sophie's father is on the council. Lord Thomise, he's so boring though; I can't imagine him being up to anything underhanded."

Auber raised an eyebrow. "It's the boring ones you have to watch. Does Sophie's gift come from her mother's side of the family or from Lord Thomise's side."

"Um, I'm not sure." Violette rubbed her temple.

"What do you know about Lord Thomise besides that he's boring?"

Violette pursed her lips. "Not much. Lord Thomise's country estate is near the south coast. His wife and son, Sophie's brother, live there. The son, Milo, manages the estate; the wife, Lady Katerina hates the capital. She only travels to the city from necessity."

"Has Sophie always lived here with her father?"

Violette tilted her head. "No, Sophie arrived three years ago. I suppose when she was old enough to leave her mother. Although, Sophie's aunt—Lord Thomise's sister— used to accompany her here often."

Auber pressed his lips together. "And what of Lord Thomise's finances? Do they have a motive to steal from King Abelaird's treasury?"

Violette shook her head. "Sophie's rich and spoiled. She has everything she wants; jewels, horses, clothes, servants. The girl lacks nothing."

"Ah... but that kind of spending requires great resources. What are Lord Thomise's holdings? The estate?"

"Lord Thomise's estate is massive. And Lord Thomise has trading rights. Their lands include a deep harbour. Lord Thomise has developed it over the years; and Milo keeps a strict eye on everything."

"Is that why Lord Thomise is on King Abelaird's council? Because of his wealth?" Auber asked, cocking his head.

Violette nodded. "Probably. Father invited him onto the council, but I don't how much he trusts Lord Thomise. It's difficult to read Lord Thomise; he doesn't speak much in council meetings."

"We need to keep our eyes on him. Does he have apartments at the castle?"

Violette shook her head. "No. He and Sophie have a house in the city. Although, now that Sophie's older, she stays in a castle guest room sometimes. If there's an event that goes late."

"Would Sophie recognize Arel?" An idea occurred to Auber.

Violette's eyes sparked with interest. "Sophie never pays attention to servants; she'd never notice her."

Auber and Violette simultaneously turned to Arel, who sighed and nodded in assent.

"It would be easier to search Sophie's chambers if I could be in there alone. I can hardly look through her things when she's sitting there."

Violette grinned. "I know just what to do."

CHAPTER 13

Two veiled figures crept through the shadowy castle garden.

One figure lugged two large canvas bags; one bag empty, one bag containing a large bulky shape.

Auber had long outgrown the small cloth bag Violette had carried him in. After procuring Auber clothes—children's short breeches and a frilly jacket, to Auber's dismay—Arel produced the canvas sack as his new mode of transport. Auber still retained froglike features; Violette feared being seen in public would cause uncomfortable questions. The canvas sack wouldn't do for everyday castle use, but for this job, it was perfect.

"I saw the nest this way." Violette led them down a little-used path through the castle orchards. They stood in an overgrown cluster of trees, black branches twisting overhead.

"There." Violette pointed to a bulge halfway up a knobbly branch. Numerous buzzing shapes whirred in and out of the hive.

"The whole nest?" Auber asked, peering at the grey mass.

"Unless you want to break the hive open," Violette answered.

Auber sighed. He had volunteered for the onerous and dangerous task of obtaining the beehive. He climbed out of his sack and Arel handed him a tin of salve, which he rubbed over every visible inch of skin.

"Are you sure this salve stuff works?" Auber asked, wrinkling his nose at the salve's noxious smell.

"The gardener assured me the salve would repel bees," Arel answered.

Auber handed the tin back to Arel.

"Fine, I'm ready."

Arel hoisted Auber to the lowest branch, and Auber began clambering up the tree. It was all right at first. A bee or two buzzed around him, suspicious about the strange smelling creature invading their territory. Auber wafted the bees away with a free hand and continued climbing.

He was close, the hive only feet away, when disaster struck. The bees, deciding as a single unit, Auber was a threat not to be tolerated, viciously attacked.

"Keep going, Auber; you're so close," Violette encouraged.

Brushing off the cloud of fierce insects, Auber climbed until he reached the hive. By now, the burgeoning number of bee stings smarted painfully. He yelped as a bee sank its stinger in the tender spot between two fingers.

Auber reached into his pocket and pulled out a cloth handkerchief, clumsily wrapping it around his hand, he used it to shove the hive from the branch.

"The hive's coming down," he shouted.

The girls jumped out of the path of the careening beehive. The second it landed, Arel lifted it with gloved hands and plopped it into the empty canvas sack.

Task completed, Auber scuttled down the tree, sliding down the last branch and tumbling to the ground.

"Ow. Ow. Ow," Auber yelled. He dived into his sack, pulling it over his head.

"I don't think that salve works," Auber said, voice muffled by the canvas.

"Are you all right, Auber?" Violette asked, hefting the sack.

"I'll be fine," Auber answered, nursing his hand. The stings were itching, swelling, and swollen.

Violette and Arel sneaked through the laundry, silent and empty this late in the evening, as the bees buzzed angrily in their canvas prison.

"Where are you planning to store the beehive?" Auber asked.

The girls responded with uncomfortable silence. They planned to release the bees when Sophie was occupied at breakfast, but breakfast wasn't for several hours.

"I know a place," Arel said. "There's a cleaning cupboard on the guest wing that hardly gets used; I'll keep the hive there."

Arel delivered Auber to his new guest chamber, a spacious room containing an actual bed. Much more comfortable than Violette's armoire. He stretched out to sleep.

****

"Auber, Auber," Arel whispered. The morning sun streamed through the windows as Auber groaned.

"Huh, what?" Auber answered, cracking his eyes open.

"We need your help. We're going to Sophie's chamber, and I need you to stand guard outside."

Auber dragged himself from the soft bed, cursing as his bare feet hit the cold floor.

"Hurry."

Arel brought him to the guest wing. Because breakfast hour had begun, it was too dangerous for Violette to accompany them. Arel deposited Auber inside an ornate credenza and left the door cracked open.

Auber watched Arel hefted the buzzing sack. Using the key Violette gave her to open the door, she slipped inside. Moments later, Arel returned empty-handed.

"Now what?" Auber whispered.

"I'll hang about here and pretend to polish the furniture. Sophie should return soon. I'll send her away, then have time to search the chamber properly. We'll tell her we need the day to clear the chamber."

"Won't the bees sting you?" Auber asked.

"Not with this," Arel answered, producing a heavy beekeepers veil.

The plan worked beautifully. At first.

As planned, Sophie returned, swanning down the corridor with a swing in her step. She flung open the door and pranced inside.

Auber watched anxiously and was rewarded when three seconds later, Sophie emerged shrieking, and flailing her arms.

"What is it?" Arel flung down her duster and approached Sophie with an air of concern.

"Bees, my room is full of horrible insects," Sophie cried.

"Oh dear. I'm so sorry, Duchess Sophie." Sophie was no duchess; giving her a higher rank was part of the plan, suggested by Violette in order to flatter Sophie into submission.

"Well." Sophie sniffed. "See that you remove the insects immediately. I'm expected back to the house later today, and I want my things packed and sent with me."

Arel curtsied. "Of course. That will be arranged. Would you like to wait in the east salon while I organise a removal?"

Sophie huffed and turned, startling a stray bee.

"Ahh." Sophie let out an unladylike yelp and darted down the corridor at an unladylike speed.

Arel watched Sophie disappear before popping on her veil and whisking into Sophie's room.

Auber remained hidden as chambermaids bustled up and down with heavy trays. The occasional lord or lady swept by in a haze of perfume and silk.

Twenty minutes later, Auber was growing bored. He was absent-mindedly watching a red-haired lady in a feathered green hat mumble to herself when something caught his eye. He pressed his eye to the crack in the credenza. Something strange was happening to the floor. He smelled a sweetness. Rose oil, Auber picked out the familiar scent. Slight dents began appearing and disappearing into the carpet along the side of the corridor. Auber narrowed his eyes and strained his ears.

A picture swayed, then stilled, as if something bumped into it, then straightened it.

Auber jumped back, hitting his head on the top of the credenza. Sophie. She must have suspected something was afoot and returned to her chamber.

He had to do something.

Auber searched the corridor with frantic eyes as Sophie approached the credenza. Panic-stricken, he flung the credenza door out, then slammed it shut again.

The dents in the carpet stopped. He must have startled Sophie enough to stop her. After a few seconds, however, the dents started again. The rose oil scent growing stronger, Auber grabbed a heavy silver candlestick and threw it.

There was a muffled shriek and a dull thud. Sophie must have bumped into the wall when Auber startled her.

Sophie's chamber door opened, and Arel emerged. Glancing around and seeing no one, Arel headed for the credenza.

Auber gulped, knowing they were going to be caught. Taking a deep breath, he croaked loudly in a low voice.

The dents in the carpet scurry away, accompanied by a nervous squeak.

Arel opened the door to the credenza. "Auber, what are you doing? Anyone might hear you in the guest wing."

Auber lowered his voice to a whisper. "We can't talk here. Sophie was in the hall, invisible. She could return any moment. We need to go immediately."

Arel gasped, glancing around. "Sophie's here now?"

"I think I scared her off, but I'm not sure."

Just as Auber was speaking, Sophie walked around the corner.

"Did you get rid of the bees?" Sophie asked, her voice held a haughty tone, but Auber glimpsed sparks of nervousness lurking in Sophie's eyes.

"I believe I need help from a gardener," Arel answered, lowering her head.

Sophie huffed.

"I can't wait all day, you know. And I'm going to need a different chamber next time I stay. This corridor gives me the creeps." She glared at the offending credenza.

Arel hid a smile as she nodded her assent, assuring Sophie she would pass the message to the head housekeeper.

Sophie swept down the corridor, and Arel lost no time, scooping Auber into his canvas sack and hurrying back to Violette's chambers.

"What did you find?" Violette asked, turning from her painting, this one of a rose garden in full bloom.

"I discovered pieces of your missing jewelry... and I found this," Arel said, holding out a metal disk the size of a coin.

"What's that? It's not very pretty," Violette said, taking the disk and examining it from all angles.

"I don't know what the talisman is, but it contains powerful magic. I can feel it."

"May I?" Auber reached for the object, touching it with a single finger. A jolt of electricity swarmed up his arm, tingling every nerve and fibre in its path. He jerked his hand away, shaking off the strange feeling.

"You can feel magic too?" Arel asked.

"Definitely magic," Auber shuddered, remembering the collection of magical artifacts in Lord Ruben's castle. This talisman had a similar feeling, and he didn't like it.

"What does the talisman do?" Violette asked, setting it on the vanity and rubbing her fingers on her paint cloth.

"I don't know. There are inscriptions, but it's a language I can't read," Arel answered.

"Let me look again?" Auber asked. His father ensured he was well versed in different languages. He peered at the script circling the edge of the coin, noticing the text seemed to shiver and swirl before his eyes. He squinted, forcing himself to concentrate until words emerged.

"It's an enhancement ward," Auber said. He pushed the coin away, head pounding.

"An enhancement what?" Violette asked, a wrinkle between her eyes.

"An enhancement ward, used to strengthen gifts. It usually only works with one person at a time. They're very expensive. My father had an enhanced ring, and no one was allowed near it."

"Your father? Who was he?" Violet asked, her head swinging up.

"Er—he was Iasian, you wouldn't know him," Auber answered.

"Iasian? Magic isn't common in Iasia. They've only recently lifted the ban on using gifts. How did your father get an artifact like that?" The adorable wrinkle re-appeared between Violette's brows.

"Father never told me how he bought the ring," Auber answered. Lord Ruben had been secretive about his magic, and Auber knew enough to realize most of his gifts and artifacts were gained through nefarious methods.

"What was your father's gift?" Violette pressed.

"Father actually didn't have a gift," Auber answered, averting his eyes. Instead, Lord Ruben had stolen other's gifts, siphoning them away after taking their lives, a fact Auber had stumbled on with horror. His protest was a prime reason Auber had fallen out of favor with Lord Ruben. The reason he was in this predicament. Auber glared at his muddy green skin.

Violette threw Auber a suspicious look, a look that told Auber she wasn't finished with the conversation. Auber sighed. He didn't want to share too much information and risk ruining his chance to break the curse.

Violette lifted the coin with a lace handkerchief and deposited it in a vanity drawer.

"Did you find anything else in Sophie's room?" Violette asked Arel.

"I found this jewelry." Arel reached into her pocket and pulled out a handful of jewelry. A heavy gold necklace with a blue stone, a collection of rings, an amber and gold broach, among other baubles. Piled together, they made a glittering heap on the vanity table.

Violette touched the amber broach, running a finger along the smooth golden stones. "I wondered where this broach was because I wanted to wear it on my cloak last Wednesday. That must mean Sophie's been in my chambers. Recently."

Auber shivered. His hearing was excellent, and he'd noticed nothing suspicious. A thought occurred to him. "Wouldn't Bane have noticed Sophie sneaking in?"

Bane heard his name and bounded over from his bed on the floor, wagging his tail and looking for attention.

Violette stroked Bane's furry head. "Sophie made a point to bring Bane treats; I guess now I know why."

"How would Sophie get a key to Violette's chambers? Did you find Violette's key in the Sophie's room?"

Arel shook her head. "I didn't see the key. Sophie probably had it on her person."

Violette pressed her lips together. "I'll have the locks changed immediately. It would be good if there was a way to do it without rousing father's suspicions. I don't want to tell him until I gather more evidence."

"I'll speak to the locksmith; he's a friend of my cousins. We can probably arrange to change the locks quietly."

"Good idea," Violette said, a smile lighting up her face.

"And we should find a way to investigate Lord Thomise's house. If Sophie's involved, he might be also."

The thought sobered everyone.

"Does King Abelaird trust Lord Thomise?" Auber asked.

Violette pressed her lips together. "I don't know."

A smart rap at the chamber door interrupted the conversation. Arel opened the door, revealing a steward holding a thick cream envelope standing ramrod straight on the other side of the door.

"An invitation for Lady Violette," the steward said, bowing low.

"Thank you," Violette said, taking the envelope. She ran a manicured fingernail along the side of the envelope and a card slid into Violette's hand, spiky masculine, handwriting scrawled across the front.

"Prince Landry wants to meet me," Violette sank slowly on the bed as panic flared in her eyes.

"Where does Prince Landry propose to meet?" Auber asked.

"For a walk in the castle gardens," Violette answered. "I can't let him see my face in this condition." Her hand reached automatically for the scar on her face, still a deep red. The skin was wrinkled with the aftermath of the incident. A tear ran down her cheek.

"I can help…" Arel said, hesitantly.

"You can, how?" Violette asked, eyes questioning.

"I have an uncle who's… gifted. He can make things appear like they're not. A bit like a ward."

Violette's eyes flooded with hope. "Can your uncle make the scars disappear?"

Arel nodded slowly. "He can… but there's a cost."

"What's the cost? I'll pay him whatever he wants," Violette said.

"There's a money cost, yes. But that's not what I mean. There's another cost, a personal cost."

Violette tipped her head, waiting for Arel to continue.

"What would Violette give up?" Auber asked.

"It's different for each person. For example, when a poor woman wanted to appear rich to marry a wealthy husband, the cost was her health. Once he changed a woman's appearance so she could hide from her violent husband."

"What was the cost for that?" Violette was at the edge of her seat.

"Her hair fell out; she ended up completely bald."

Violette grimaced, touching her shiny brunette tresses. "Could I at least talk to your uncle? It might be worth it if Landry is as interested as he appears."

Arel nodded. "I'll see if I can find him. He hangs about in the old quarter markets."

"The old quarter, where mage market is?" Violette asked, eyes sparking with interest.

CHAPTER 14

The unmarked carriage rolled toward the old quarter, where teetering buildings loomed on each side of the narrow cobblestone street, casting dark shadows over the rumbling carriage. Violette had the sense to take two guards, one placed on either end of the carriage. Auber drew back the curtain. Piles of refuse lay in rotting piles, drawing clouds of buzzing flies to their noxious odor. The few people around scurried by, glancing furtively at the rattling carriage.

No one went to old quarter mage market without good reason.

Auber had never been in a city. The sights and smells overwhelmed him with their intensity.

The old quarter was quiet. Ominous.

The carriage rolled to a stop outside a covered market.

"Is this the mage market?" Violette adjusted her veil so she could peek out.

Arel nodded, her mouth pressed in a thin line. "Follow me and do exactly what I say. And for goodness sake, don't let anyone know you're carrying money, and especially don't let anyone see you're the princess."

"What should I do?" Auber asked. He didn't fancy being trundled into the increasingly restrictive sack again.

Arel shrugged. "You can walk; no one will look twice here."

They descended from the carriage, Violette looking around in interest. She had dressed in an old maid's uniform covered with a patched cloak; her dark glossy hair was bundled under a kerchief. Auber scampered to keep up as the two girls entered the worn set of wooden double doors.

Auber gaped. Despite the quiet street, the market bustled with activity. Stalls lined the wide building; each vender displaying their wares. Some venders had no wares, just a sign revealing the service offered.

"Follow me," Arel whispered. "Uncle Morem's stall is this way." She strode down a narrow aisle. Throwing a longing glance at the tantalising wares, Violette followed, with Auber close behind.

As Arel predicted, no one looked twice at Auber. If he were perfectly honest, he was the least strange thing in the mage market. He skipped away as a snake reared its head from a colourful basket and swayed, beady eyes fixed on Auber's form.

"Try to keep up," Arel whispered, her body taut with tension. She headed for the far south corner of the market, where a ramshackle stall covered with a grimy cloth leaned against the wall. The table held a mortar and pestle, along with an array of ingredients. Auber recognized some herbs and roots from his father's workroom at the castle.

"Uncle Morem?" Arel whispered, tapping the table.

Auber stared at the stall. There was no one there.

"Uncle Morem, I know you're here," Arel whispered again, louder this time.

The grimy cloth rustled. A disheveled head popped out. "Yes, child." Uncle Morem climbed from underneath the stall, stretching and yawning. He flicked a strand of long greasy hair from his eyes.

"Uncle Morem, what have we told you about sleeping here. It's not safe," Arel scolded.

"Sorry. I get sleepy though." Uncle Morem picked at a black line of grime under his fingernail. "Anyway, Arel, what brings you here? I thought you had a fancy job at the castle."

"Oh yes. I need your help. For a.... friend." Arel glanced uneasily toward Violette, who stepped forward.

Uncle Morem ran his eyes over Violette. "Help? What do you need me to do?" he asked.

"Not much, we need a glamour ward."

Uncle Morem narrowed his eyes. "You know those aren't allowed. Because of..." he lowered his voice to a whisper. "The cost."

"That won't be a problem," Violette said, voice clear and confident.

Uncle Morem threw Violette a suspicious glance. "Silly girl, you don't know what the cost is."

Violette shrugged. "This ward is more important. There's a lot at stake, so can you do it?"

Uncle Morem's eyes glittered. "Glamour wards aren't cheap. I'll need gold in advance because I'm putting myself at risk."

"Whatever you want," Violette answered, giving Uncle Morem a crisp nod.

Arel threw Violette a horrified look. "You're supposed to bargain," she said.

"It's fine," Violette said. "Pay the man what he wants."

Uncle Morem nodded, his face taking on a serious expression. "Show me what you need done," he said.

Violette glanced around the market. Seeing they were in a quiet area, she lifted a corner of her veil for Uncle Morem to see.

"Ah. You wish to be returned to your former skin?" Uncle Morem asked.

Violette nodded, letting the veil fall securely into place.

"How long do you need the ward to hold? Glamour wards are only temporary," Uncle Morem said.

The three exchanged glances. This was something they hadn't discussed.

"How long can you build the glamour ward to last?" Violette asked.

Uncle Morem shrugged. "Three weeks?"

"Done," Violette agreed.

Springing into action, Uncle Morem's hands flashed across the table. He threw an array of herbs and other ingredients into his mortar. Muttering, he crushed them, releasing a heady aroma that wafted through the air, tickling Auber's nose with a vaguely familiar scent. A scent that reminded Auber of his father.

"What about that one?" Uncle Morem jerked his head toward Auber. "Does he want his former skin glamoured?"

Auber's eyes widened in surprise; he should have realized Uncle Morem would see the Lord Ruben's curse. He shook his head.

"I'm all right," Auber answered.

Uncle Morem inclined his head and continued mixing. When he finished, he scooped the greeny grey mixture into a glass vial stoppered with a cork.

"Take this tincture before bed for best results."

Violette took the bottle, the slight tremble in her hand the only sign of her nervousness. "And what about the cost?" she asked.

Uncle Morem twisted his lip. "You won't know until it happens. Whatever it is, it will be soon," he answered.

Violette nodded, reaching in her purse for the gold coins Uncle Morem required. His grimy paw closed around them greedily.

"Good luck." Uncle Morem's deep black eyes gleamed. "And feel free to come back if you need anything else, niece."

Arel nodded once before leading them back to the coach, Violette clutching the precious vial in white-knuckled hands.

Heavy silence settled over the carriage on the return to the castle, each person lost in their own thoughts. The moment they arrived in Violette's chambers, she rushed straight to the vanity and ripped off her veil.

"Quick. Put the tincture on me before I lose my nerve," she said, thrusting the vial toward Arel.

"Are you sure you want to use Uncle Morem's glamour ward? There might a better way."

Violette bit her lip. "No. I have to marry Prince Landry if I want to save Luixe. It will be fine. Landry is pleasant and kind and the Iasians will help pull the castle out of debt. Father will be pleased," she answered, her face pale.

Arel hesitated before carefully uncorking the vial, pouring the liquid onto a fine brush. Violette tilted her head and Arel began to apply the mixture.

Three pairs of anxious eyes stared at Violette's face. With mingled relief and dismay, Auber watched the crinkled skin turn smooth and creamy, blending perfectly with the rest of Violette's face. Auber caught his breath, a twinge shooting through his chest as saw the full extent of Violette's beauty. How could he possibly think he could attract someone like that? Even in his human state, he wouldn't have a chance.

Violette reached a tentative hand and touched her cheek, running a finger toward her smooth neck. "I can't believe the tincture worked, and there's enough for three weeks?" she said, a wide smile lighting up her face.

"Yes, if you apply regularly and use it carefully. But the most important matter is, how do you feel?" Arel asked. Her troubled eyes studied Violette, as if expecting her to disappear at any moment.

"I feel good," Violette answered.

Arel's eyes didn't lose their shadows, and Auber knew she was thinking of the price. The unpaid price and wondering what it would be.

"I can't wait to show everyone," Violette flitted to the dressing room. "What should I wear? Oh, and I must reply to Prince Landry's invitation." She scampered to the writing desk, pulling out thick ivory coloured stationary. "Hmm... what should I say?" she dipped her pen in the inkwell and scrawled a few lines. "There." Violette blew the ink dry and sealed the letter with a blob of bright red wax. "Now for the dress." She floated to the dressing room.

Auber and Arel exchanged an anxious glance.

"Violette," Auber hesitated. "Do you think it's a good idea to go wandering around the castle? People talk. The visitors don't know you were scarred. But everyone else will wonder what happened."

Violette froze. "You think I should stay in my room?" she asked, the smile sliding from her face.

Auber nodded.

Violette turned to Arel. "And you too?"

Arel reluctantly agreed. "At least until you make progress with Prince Landry. Do you want your father to ask questions? You know what he thinks of that particular kind of magic."

Violette flopped on the bed. "Another secret," she said, pressing a hand over her eyes and groaning. "I know you're right."

"I understand," Auber said, placing a cautious hand on Violette's shoulder.

Violette closed her eyes and took a deep breath. "I suppose you're right," she said, sitting up.

Violette stayed in her room painting that afternoon, only leaving veiled to take Bane for a brief walk in the castle gardens. Her meeting with Landry took place the next morning. The dressing room was a mess. Discarded dresses lay across every surface; jewelry spilled out of the cases and shoes scattered across the floor.

"I need to make everything perfect," Violette said, trying on a pair of velvet slippers. She turned her foot, examining it from every angle. "Maybe leather slippers are better; the grass might be damp." She kicked the velvet slippers off, sliding into a soft leather pair Arel held out to her.

"That's better. Wish me luck!"

Violette shoved a veiled hat over her head and left.

"Should we go keep an eye on her?" Auber asked, shifting his gaze to the door, worrying about the chaos of Violette's nerves.

"Probably." Arel busied herself smoothing wrinkles from a green satin dress before hanging it up.

Auber pulled at the waistband of his trousers and sucked in a breath. The trousers were tight, making it difficult to breathe.

"Do you need a bigger set of clothes already?" Arel asked, scanning Auber's form.

Auber glanced down, noticing the gaping buttons on his jacket. "I guess I do," he answered, stretching out a hand to examine it. The skin was now only slightly green. He now walked easily on two legs, and could pass for a bilious, odd-looking child.

"I can watch Violette, if you have work to do," Auber volunteered. Arel hung up another dress, folding the matching velvet wrap.

"Are you sure?"

Auber nodded. He needed to catch up with Therese, anyway. He felt terrible for neglecting her over the past few days.

Shoving a servant's cap low over his head, Auber grabbed a tray before walking down the servant's corridors and heading for the gardens. Hiding the tray behind a potted plant, he replaced them with a pair of gardening shears. If anyone asked, he would pretend to be a servant gathering flowers for his mistress.

Auber strode across the grass toward Violette's favourite spot, a gazebo overlooking the pond. Hidden behind a stand of trees, it offered privacy from casual castle visitors. Auber trod carefully across the grass, spotting Violette's pale blue dress and feathered hat perching next to Prince Landry's tall figure.

A fiery bolt of jealousy shot through Auber as tinkling laughter floated through the air.

Prince Landry must be hilarious, Auber thought bitterly, shooting the Iasian prince a fierce glare. The garden was quiet this early in the morning. Only a few other visitors strolled the grounds, keeping their distance from the prince and princess. Auber crept closer, eying a nearby rosebush. Maybe he should cut a few roses to keep his cover intact. He snicked a large peach hued blossom.

A giggle prickled Auber's ears. Violette was fluttering her lashes at Prince Landry, who responded with an affable grin. Auber glowered at the roses, wincing as another giggle floated through the air. Prince Landry wasn't that funny. Violette was edging closer to the prince, and Auber gritted his teeth, clenching the rose tight in his fist. A stabbing pain sliced through his hand. He looked down. A thorn had pierced his finger, a drop of blood welling up.

Suddenly, sharp blinding pain speared through every inch of his body. He stared at his hand in horror; it was turning dark green, rubbery skin and webbing replacing his near human flesh.

No, no, no. Not after all the progress I made. Auber stared in mingled dread and disgust as his fingers grew webs. The secateurs thudded to the earth; he was shrinking rapidly. Auber cursed to himself as he glanced at the prince and princess, hoping they hadn't heard his low cry.

They were kissing.

Auber was back to his original size and shape. An ordinary green pond frog. He shivered under a leaf, body spasming from its ordeal.

He peeked out. If only he hadn't encouraged Violette to pursue Prince Landry. He had been so confident the curse was failing and his recent changes would continue. He didn't have time to start breaking the curse again. And he didn't want to. Auber realized this with a jolt of clarity. He wanted Violette.

Discouraged and disheartened, Auber hopped over his discarded clothing. Keeping hidden in the hedges and flowerbeds, he made his way slowly back to the castle.

After trial and error, Auber found his way back to the royal wing. He waited behind a flowing drape until Violette returned, flushed and triumphant from her successful meeting with Prince Landry. Violette hummed as she fitted her shiny new key into the lock.

"Wait for me," Auber said, hopping in after her.

"What happened to you?" Violette peered down at Auber with puzzled eyes.

"I don't want to talk about it," Auber answered, hopping across the plush carpet and plunking into his favourite window seat. Bane got up and nosed him curiously before settling back on his cushion.

"All right." Violette swanned to the vanity and admired herself in the mirror. "Well? Aren't you going to ask about Prince Landry?" she asked, fluffing her hair.

"I don't need to ask," Auber replied. "I can see Prince Landry was nice." He softened. *None of this is Violette's fault,* he reminded himself. *She doesn't know the details of the curse.*

Violette turned to Auber, a tender expression creeping into her eyes. "I'm sorry. You were making so much progress with your curse. Are you sure you don't want to tell me what happened? Maybe I can help."

Auber shook his head. "No. I don't think you can. And I'm happy for you, truly. Now, tell me about Prince Landry," he said, forcing the last sentence out of his mouth with reluctance.

Violette's face broke into a beaming smile. "Prince Landry is lovely, funny, kind. I really think this match might work. Father will be so pleased. That reminds me, I must speak to Father and update him before this afternoon's council meeting. Do you want to come along?"

"All right," Auber said. "But how are you going to hide your glamour from him?"

A shadow crossed Violette's face. "I'll wear a veil, I suppose."

"Really?" Auber stared at her. "After all this time, you're starting to wear a veil? Won't King Abelaird be suspicious?"

Violette chewed her lip thoughtfully. "I suppose I could put something on it. Pretend it's a new salve?" She moved some jars and pots around on her vanity. "This one." She held a green glass jar. "It should cover everything just fine."

Auber watched as Violette smeared a thick paste over her cheek and neck. "There, that should hide it. Let's go, you'll fit in the bag now that you're small again." Violette opened the bag for Auber to climb in.

"Come in." King Abelaird sat at his polished desk, a half filled glass tumbler at his elbow. "Violette, how lovely to see you."

"Hello, Father." Violette removed her veil.

"A new salve, darling? Hopefully, this one works a little better." King Abelaird eyed the sticky substance covering Violette's cheek.

"Yes, Father," Violette answered, lowering her eyes.

King Abelaird's face softened. "Well. Have you got news for me? Any success from the masked ball?" he asked.

"Actually." Violette took a seat on the settee. "There was one interesting suitor at the masked ball."

King Abelaird leaned forward, threading his fingers together. "Who is it?"

"Prince Landry of Iasia," Violette answered, raising her head high.

"We'll have to move fast then. Sophie is after Prince Landry too."

"Do you mean Sophie, Lord Thomise's daughter?" Violette asked.

King Abelaird nodded, fingering his glass.

"Surely, he can ask Sophie to back off," Violette said.

King Abelaird gazed thoughtfully at his hands. "At one time, I thought so. But Lord Thomise has proved difficult as of late."

"How?" Violette questioned, pressing for more information. "Lord Thomise never defies you in council meetings."

"True, but that doesn't mean he doesn't influence people. Lord Thomise comes from a powerful family with vast resources. Sometimes I wonder if he's the ally I assumed he was."

Violette pressed her lips together, her eyes troubled.

"Do you trust Lord Thomise?" Violette asked. "I've noticed Sophie is a bit.... odd. I think she may be gifted."

King Abelaird looked up, surprised. "What makes you think that? Gifts run in their family, but Lord Thomise has never mentioned a gift in connection with Sophie." King Abelaird picked up his glass tumbler and gulped.

Violette hesitated, debating whether she should share her suspicions. But before she could open her mouth, King Abelaird clutched his chest, his face draining of colour.

"Father, are you all right?" Violette sprung from her seat.

"Just catching my breath." King Abelaird took a deep, shuddering breath as his face creased in pain.

Violette put a hand to King Abelaird's pale forehead. "Where does it hurt?"

"Here." King Abelaird gasped, rubbing his chest with a shaking hand. "If you could just get me my tonic. The vial in the drinks cabinet."

Violette flew to the drinks cabinet, throwing the doors open.

"Is it this?" she snatched an amber glass vial half full of a clear liquid.

King Abelaird nodded. "Mix it with water."

With trembling hands, Violette poured water from the carafe into a glass.

"Here." The water slopped over the edge of the glass as she handed it to her father.

King Abelaird drank deeply, relaxing as the tonic burned through his bloodstream.

"Better?" Violette asked, hovering anxiously over King Abelaird.

King Abelaird nodded. Although beads of sweat lined his forehead, color was returning to his face.

"How many attacks have you had?" Violette returned to the settee.

"Not many." King Abelaird's eyes slid away. "That's the worst one yet."

Violette stared at the floor, blinking.

King Abelaird sighed. "Don't look like that. It's not that serious; I hate you to worry."

"Are these attacks why you're rushing to marry me off the to the nearest suitor?" Violette asked, raising her eyes to her father.

King Abelaird shook his head. "No, well, maybe a little."

Violette tossed her hair, glaring at her father. "I can take care of myself, you know."

King Abelaird sighed. "I know, but I want you to be safe. To have someone to share the burden of ruling. It's difficult reigning alone. My council is good, but I'm afraid..."

"Afraid of what, that the council won't listen to me? That they won't respect me?"

King Abelaird averted his eyes. "You're young. If there's two ruling, the council would have to listen."

Violette plucked at the lace on her sleeve. "I see. Well, speaking of your council," she said, taking a deep breath. "I'm worried about Lord Thomise and Sophie. I think Sophie has access to places she shouldn't go."

King Abelaird's head shot up. "What makes you think that?"

"You know that frog you gave me?"

King Abelaird nodded, waiting for Violette to continue.

Violette filled her father in on what Auber had seen, watching as King Abelaird's face grew gave with concern.

"If this is true, Lord Thomise has far deeper designs than pilfering a few shiny baubles. He's grown in influence in court, especially with the help of Sophie to sway the younger generation. Sophie has refused all suitors, and I believe Lord Thomise has been dangling her, hoping to gain interest. Sophie's inheritance comes with a rich dowry— lands, wealth, resources."

Violette's eyes were troubled. "What do you think Lord Thomise's plans are?"

King Abelaird pressed his lips together. "If Lord Thomise is behind whoever is siphoning from the treasury, he may be planning to take over the kingdom."

Violette gasped. "Can he do that?"

"With me out of the way, it's possible," King Abelaird said, eyes growing cold. "But we have no proof. If—and I say if. If this is Lord Thomise's plan, he's cautious and slow, biding his time until the exact right moment arrives."

"We have to stop him," Violette said, clenching her hands together on her knee, her knuckles turning white against her skin.

King Abelaird leaned back. "I'll speak to the spymaster. We'll plant someone in his house. Someone to watch him."

Violette narrowed her eyes. "How long will that take?"

King Abelaird shook his head. "I don't know. Lord Thomise will be extremely careful and he's obviously prepared. We'll to have to wait until he slips. Now, tell me, what progress have you made with Prince Landry? Perhaps the Iasian alliance is our best chance of opposing Lord Thomise."

After much discussion, Violette left King Abelaird's study with an air of dissatisfaction.

"It will take forever to plant someone in Lord Thomise's house, and then we have to wait until they gain his trust and stumble across useful information," Violette complained, flopping on her bed.

"Maybe I could help," Auber said.

"You?" Violette's head swung up.

Auber hopped over the bedcovers. "Think about it. If I go to Lord Thomise's house as I am presently, I would have the run of his entire estate, access to any chamber, privy to every conversation."

Violette hesitated. "But it would be dangerous. What if someone caught you? They would either think you were a garden frog and.... dispose of you. Or if you started talking, they would suspect you're a spy. No, if Lord Thomise is a traitor, it's better if you don't go near him."

Auber hopped onto a frilly satin cushion. "Violette, listen to me. You don't have many options. This is your best chance to learn what Lord Thomise is up to. I could listen to everything, find the documents, then sneak out."

Violette closed her eyes, leaning against a stack of pillows.

"I suppose. But I still don't like it." Violette said with a frown. "Just promise me that if you're in any danger, you'll step back immediately."

Auber nodded. "I promise."

CHAPTER 15

Arel strolled along the long tree-lined avenue, a cloth covered market basket slung over one arm. A kerchief covered her hair, and she was dressed in tattered peasant clothes.

"Almost there," she whispered.

Auber attempted to peer through the chinks in the basket. The only thing he saw was grass. The gentle swing of the basket made his queasy stomach seize.

"Now remember, I'll meet you in exactly two days," Arel instructed. She stopped at a gigantic wrought-iron gate and set the market basket down, stretching and rubbing her back as if pausing to rest.

"Oy, what are you doing, miss?" a roughly dressed gardener glanced up from the flowerbed he was digging.

"Sorry, I'm just passing by. I had to collect some apples at the market for my mistress," Arel answered, tilting her head.

"Well, move along, no loitering near Lord Thomise's gates." The gardener returned to his digging. Auber glimpsed silver hanging at the gardener's side. An armed guard, he realized. Lord Thomise took no chances. He slipped out of the market basket and huddled in a clump of grass.

"Good luck," Arel whispered, picking up the empty basket and continuing down the lane.

Auber crouched low, considering his next move. The tree lined drive led to a stately manor of finely dressed stone. Purple smoke rose from the chimney into the clear blue sky. The front entrance was firmly closed. Auber began hopping through the long grass edging the drive. He would try the kitchen door.

Hours later, after a close call with a cat—Auber was forced to nestle inside a flowerpot until the feline grew bored and wandered off—Auber reached the kitchen courtyard. It was empty save a single maid emptying a bucket of scrubbing water. Auber slipped around the edge of the courtyard, keeping to the deep shadows. He hopped over the threshold into the kitchen, hiding at the bottom of the firewood pile.

Now to find a way into Lord Thomise's study, Auber thought, waiting for an opportunity to slip into the rest of the house.

After lunch, the maids left, but to Auber's dismay, the cook remained pottering with the bread baking. Auber realized he would have to leave now. Creeping along the wall and keeping under the furniture when possible, he reached the half-open door and slipped out.

The servant's corridor stretched before him, long and dimly lit, with a staircase rising at the end. Auber sighed as the staircase loomed before him. Lord Thomise's private chambers were probably at the top of the house. Heart in his chest, Auber struggled up the stairs, breathing a sigh of relief when he reached the top. The door was cracked open; Auber peered through the crack. A polished floor dotted with plush rugs stretched before him. Gold framed paintings lined the walls. This must be Lord Thomise's quarters. Bolstered by this discovery, and by the abundance of hiding places, Auber rested behind a tall vase to wait.

The corridor doors on this corridor were all shut tight. Auber cursed his small size; he would have to wait until someone opened them. He didn't have to wait long. Heavy footsteps were coming his way. Auber peered around the vase. Four polished leather shoes and two finely woven pairs of breeches were headed his way. He watched Lord Thomise and a companion enter the third chamber on the left, closing the door with a solid thud. Auber heard murmuring voices rise and fall.

This was useless. He had to get closer to understand. Next to the chamber, a huge polished mirror leaned against the wall. Auber crept behind the mirror, trying to ignore the unpleasant tang of magic that clung to its shining surface. Ugh. It reminded him of his father, and not in a good way.

Auber leaned toward the chamber, straining his ears, trying to hear what the men were saying.

"... We're running out of time. Abelaird's pushing Violette toward the Iasian alliance. You know if they're on Violette's side it will compromise everything we've worked for."

"Yes, but with King Abelaird in play, the people won't take our side. How did Violette become viable after her accident? I thought Sophie had her taken care of."

"Violette must be receiving assistance. I'll get Sophie to find out." This man's voice was slightly accented. Southern, that must be Lord Thomise.

"What's the situation with the treasury?"

Lord Thomise's companion gave a mocking laugh. "Sophie's work, she's fantastic. It took King Abelaird forever to notice the coffers diminishing. And Abelaird insisted on the masked ball. Good job planting that idea in his head. The expense alone will go in our favour."

"Not if Violette snags Prince Landry," Lord Thomise said.

Auber wished he could see the other man's face. If the man was from King Abelaird's council, he would recognize him.

"What about the army? Have our plants been effective?" Lord Thomise asked.

"They report increasing discontent. I've ensured some payments went astray. The way to a man's heart is through his purse. A few weeks of unrest and the army will turn."

"See that they do," Lord Thomise was firm. "Now, I'll show you the maps. I've marked out the outposts most likely to be on the side. It's a shame Sophie couldn't do more with Landry. Violette is more capable than I thought."

Auber's gut soured. Things were worse than he thought. The men continued discussing outposts and numbers as Auber soaked in every detail, all the while, feeling the uncomfortable itch of magic seep from the mirror.

The doorknob rattled; Auber pressed himself against the mirror, heart thudding against his ribcage.

"Not long now, and you'll be living in the royal castle," Lord Thomise's comrade said, throwing the corridor with a dismissive glance. "Although this place isn't bad. You've collected some nice artifacts."

"Not all the one's I want," Lord Thomise answered.

"Ahh.. the sceptre. Didn't Sophie find it yet?"

Lord Thomise shook his head. "The sceptre must be stored in King Abelaird's private collection. He's the only one with a key."

The men continued down the corridor, Auber watching as they disappeared around the corner. Skin buzzing from the proximity of the mirror, Auber emerged from his hiding place, stretching to examine over the mirror's heavy frame. It looked like something his father would have coveted. The magic washed over him in waves, but all Auber saw was his own reflection peering back at him. He looked closer, then shuddered as the silver surface shivered.

Auber didn't have time to attempt cracking the mirror's secrets because footsteps— a single set this time— were returning up the corridor. He slithered behind the mirror again; he had to be careful. Lord Thomise was a dangerous man.

Lord Thomise paused in front of the mirror.

"Show me Violette," he said in a commanding voice

Silence ticked by as Lord Thomise stood in front of the mirror. Auber couldn't hear anything, but after a few minutes stretched by, Lord Thomise cursed, retreating into his chamber and slamming the door.

So that's how the mirror worked. Auber listened carefully as Lord Thomise banged around in the chamber. Papers shuffled, a chair squeaked. Auber took a deep breath and crept around to face the mirror.

Once again, only rubbery green skin and liquid eyes stared back. Auber took a deep breath.

"Show me Violette," Auber said, intensely aware of the presence in the next room.

The mirror shivered, its surface clouding as Auber stared into its depths. The murky haze cleared. A shiver raced across Auber's skin. Violette was walking through the gardens, again accompanied by Prince Landry. Auber stared hungrily at the mirror. This time, his view was unencumbered by distance and long grass. A sharp pain pierced Auber's chest as Violette leaned close to Prince Landry, who was showing her something he held in his hand. Auber glared at his green skin.

How could I hope to compete with a handsome prince? Auber thought bitterly. His heart clenched as Landry brushed a lock of hair from Violette's eyes. A rustle in the next room dragged his attention from the mirror. He returned to his hiding place just as Lord Thomise barged out, shouting for a messenger.

I have to get into that study, Auber thought, eyeing Lord Thomise's shining black shoes. He edged closer to the door. Lord Thomise was facing away from him. Auber took the chance and ran, silent, webbed feet rushing across the carpet and into the chamber.

Auber spotted a marble statue of a woman holding a basket of grapes. The perfect hiding place. He dashed across the chamber, ducking behind the statue a single second before Lord Thomise reappeared.

Lord Thomise strode across the room, sitting at the massive wooden desk by the window. Auber peeked around the plinth, watching closely as Lord Thomise leafed through a stack of parchments, muttering to himself. His stomach growled as time stretched out and Lord Thomise showed no inclination of leaving.

What is in those parchments? Auber wondered.

Surely, they held the key to Lord Thomise's traitorous plans. Shadows lengthened, and a chambermaid lit the lamps and stoked the fires, asking Lord Thomise if he planned to dine with lady Sophie that evening.

"I have much work to do," Lord Thomise's accented voice answered. "Lady Sophie will dine here in my chamber tonight." The chambermaid bobbed a curtsy.

Presently, Sophie arrived in a flurry of silk and perfume.

"Hello, Father." She leaned down, brushing a dry kiss against the stern face.

"Sophie. I heard news."

"What news, Father?" Sophie answered, head held high, however the slight tremble in her voice revealed her fears.

"Prince Landry is pursuing the Princess." Lord Thomise's voice was edged with anger; he frowned.

Sophie tinkled a laugh. "Father. You can't possibly think Violette could attract the prince. They've been walking... in the garden. But the princess remains veiled. When Prince Landry sees the princess, and he will, he'll change his mind."

Hm.... Sophie doesn't know about Violette's glamour ward, Auber thought, leaning forward.

Lord Thomise pinned his daughter with a stern look. "That's not what I saw."

"What did you see, Father?" Sophie asked, clenching her hands in her lap.

"I saw her face. It was perfect. Unblemished. Beautiful."

"But... how?" Sophie's cheeks tinged pink. "I replaced evert salve in Violette's chambers. It's not possible Violette's scars could heal."

"Are you sure she's using the salves you planted?" Lord Thomise's voice was hard.

"Of course, I replaced or changed every single salve and tincture. That wasn't cheap, by the way."

Lord Thomise raised an eyebrow. "What I saw was Violette, flawless, with Prince Landry. I thought you were taking care of Violette. You're slipping. You know what will happen when you're no longer useful."

Sophie's face drained of colour, her head bowed. "Of course, Father. I won't fail," she answered in a low voice.

"See that you don't."

The maid delivering food interrupted them. Auber's stomach clenched at the delicious smells floating through the air. Roast beef, rich gravy, delicate herbs.

Lord Thomise waited until the maid left.

"Well, Sophie?" Lord Thomise tapped an impatient finger on the desk.

"I'm very sorry for my failure, Father. I'll find Prince Landry and see that he doesn't approach Princess Violette again."

Lord Thomise nodded. "And how will you accomplish this feat?"

Sophie swallowed. "I'll give Prince Landry whatever he wants—at any cost."

"You know what's at stake?" Lord Thomise speared an asparagus tip.

"I know." Sophie sounded defeated, small.

"Good. You're dismissed."

Auber watched as Sophie left her full plate, gliding out of the room, closing the door softly behind her.

Lord Thomise finished his dinner in silence, then sat at his desk long after, reading papers and writing messages. Auber wondered if he was ever going to leave.

Finally, the fire burned low, and Lord Thomise set down his quill, scraping his chair back. Taking the lamp with him, he left the chamber, locking the door behind him.

Auber scooted from behind his hiding place. To his extreme disappointment, the maid had collected the plates, trailing the scent of gravy and roast beef behind her as she exited the chamber.

After trial and error, Auber clambered onto Lord Thomise's desk by scrambling onto the slippery leather chair and hopping onto the slick, polished surface. The dying embers cast enough light for Auber to see parchments spread across the desk.

At last. Auber examined the stacks of parchments and ledgers surrounding him. Wondering where to start. He nudged a ledger, watching it slide down the stack, landing with a thump. A matching thump sounded outside the door.

Auber froze as a shaft of light streaked across the patterned rug. What was that?

Lord Thomise strode into the chamber. Auber's heart thumped. There was nowhere to hide. He crouched against the ledgers, hoping to blend with the shadows as Lord Thomise scanned the desk, frowning.

"How did that happen?" Lord Thomise muttered, frowning as he righted the fallen ledger. Auber's heart squeezed as Lord Thomise looked suspiciously around before being satisfied there was nothing else amiss. He grabbed a slim brown book before leaving the chamber again.

Auber waited as the fear drained from his bones. That was a close call—too close. Keeping one eye on the door, Auber was grateful for his amphibian night vision. What to human eyes was a mass of shadows, to Auber was pin sharp, colorful detail. He awkwardly shuffled parchments with his webbed feet, searching for something—anything—to show evidence of Lord Thomise treachery.

The papers mostly pertained to the running of the estate. Auber's eyes widened at the extent of Lord Thomise's holdings. He'd judged from their position in court and Sophie's relaxed attitude toward expenditures they were wealthy, but this was something else. Auber tucked the information away as he continued his search. When nothing turned up, he sat back on his haunches, scanning the chamber, searching for a hiding place. A cunning man like Lord Thomise would keep his plans out of sight, safe from the curious eyes of household staff. Auber eyes lighted on a locked cabinet behind the desk.

Now to find a key.

Auber flicked open the inlaid silver box that stood on the desk. A collection of keys stared back at him. Which one? His eyes flicked to the locked cabinet. Bronze and small.

He searched through the keys, finding three likely candidates. He slipped them into his cheek before climbing down from his unwieldy perch. Auber sat on the chair. He would have to stretch to reach the cabinet. Somehow, he eased each key into the lock. The second key fit. Mingled hope and apprehension shot through Auber as he twisted. With a metallic click, the lock popped, and the door swung open.

Neat stacks of parchment met Auber's gaze. He looked at the top page, a thrill running through him as he realized this was it.

Auber read each page, carefully committing the information to memory before he pushed the cabinet door shut. Now to return the key. Lord Thomise was already suspicious; Auber knew Lord Thomise wouldn't hesitate to move or destroy the documents if he had a ghost of a suspicion something was amiss. After returning everything to its original position, Auber hopped down from the desk.

Now to watch and wait.

It was a long, thirsty, hungry day.

Auber managed to sip some lukewarm tea from a forgotten cup and skim scone crumbs from the carpet, but it wasn't until evening that he managed his escape. When the maid arrived to replenish the coal, Auber crept out the chamber door and scurried behind the mirror, hiding from the butler who stalked the corridor with Lord Thomise's messages. He breathed a sigh of relief as the butler's footsteps faded down the staircase.

Finally, late that afternoon, Auber picked through the smooth grass lawn at Lord Thomise's front gate. The shadows had lengthened; the light was gold with late afternoon sun.

Auber hoped he hadn't missed Arel. His stomach growled as he eyed a fly that buzzed lazily around the flowerbed. Ugh. He turned his head away.

The sky was purple before Arel came up the garden path. She set her basket next to the gate and rubbed her lower back, pretending to rest.

"About time you arrived," Auber grumbled, climbing into the basket.

"Oh hush. I was here earlier, and that gardener chased me off. I couldn't make him suspicious by returning too soon," Arel said, picking up the basket with Auber tucked safely inside.

"You brought food?" Auber asked, immediately forgiving Arel's lateness.

"Yes. I wasn't sure what you were eating in there. I figured you'd be in Lord Thomise's study."

"That's right, I'm starving," Auber said, nibbling a slice of ham.

Half an hour later, Auber was settling on Violette's pillow. She had reapplied Uncle Morem's salve, both cheeks displaying flawless, unblemished skin.

"What did you find at Lord Thomise's estate?" Violette asked, giving Auber an eager look.

"We were right about Lord Thomise. He's a traitor."

Violette sucked in a breath. "He is?"

Auber nodded. "And that's not all. He's using Sophie to spy, and a magic mirror as well."

Violette drew her brows together, tilting her head.

"A magic mirror that shows you anything you ask. At least, I think it does. I couldn't exactly ask Lord Thomise for a demonstration."

"Can the mirror hear us or just see us?"

"I heard nothing, so the mirror must just see us. I tried it when no one was looking, but I ran out of time," Auber answered with a shiver of distaste as he remembered the strong metallic tang of magic surrounding the mirror.

"What else did you learn?"

"Our suspicions were correct. Lord Thomise is trying to bankrupt the castle so he can take over Luixe."

"Take over from father?"

Auber shook his head. "Take over from you. I don't think he plans for your father to be around."

Violette's eyes flashed. "That's years away!"

Auber hesitated, heart sinking.

"Oh. I see." Violette pressed her lips into a thin angry line, her knuckles gripping the cushion she held on her lap. "How did Lord Thomise plan to do it?"

Auber shrugged. "I couldn't find his plans. I doubt he has them in writing, too risky, even for him."

"You must have a suspicion—poison?"

Auber nodded. "That's my best guess."

Violette's eyes shadowed. "Do you think he's started... administering it? Is that why father's ill?" Violette began pacing the rug. Bane, sensing Violette's distress, whined from his bed in the corner.

"We have to stop him," Violette whirled to face Auber. "We have to stop Sophie."

Auber hesitated, "There is one thing they want. Lord Thomise seemed quite determined to get it."

"What is it?" Violette asked, eyes glittering.

"The sceptre. Lord Thomise had Sophie look for it in the treasury, but she couldn't find it. He think's it's in King Abelaird's private collection."

"Couldn't Lord Thomise find the sceptre with his mirror?" Violette's eyes narrowed.

"I guess not; maybe the mirror has limitations."

"We need to learn what the mirror's limitations are. But we'll worry about that later. I know where father keeps the sceptre." Violette cast a cautious glance around the room. "I don't want to say it out loud.... Just in case. Let me get ready and we'll take this to father," she said, her lips pressed together.

Violette sat at her vanity, opening a jar of salve.

"Stop," Auber said.

Violette dropped the silver lid with a clatter. "What?"

"The salves, Lord Thomise had Sophie replace them or alter them. With something that makes your scars worse."

Violette dropped the jar of salve with a thump. "That sneaky little snake. I knew I didn't like her for a reason. How dare she... Arel?"

"Yes?" Arel poked her head around the corner. She had been busy at the never-ending task of tidying Violette's dressing room.

"Get me a basket."

Auber watched as Violette swept every single jar and vial of salves and concoctions into the basket. "There," she said, dusting her hands. "We'll replace them; with the new key, it's impossible for Sophie to tamper with them."

"Violette?" Arel asked, voice tentative.

"Yes," Violette replied, stroking Bane's head.

"Didn't Auber say Lord Thomise was watching in the mirror?"

Violette nodded.

"If Lord Thomise sees you destroy the salves, he'll suspect something."

"Oh, I hadn't thought of that." Realization dawned in Violette's eyes. "Very well. Put the salves back on the vanity. But if I ever catch that little rat... I'll... I'll.. I don't know what I'll do, but it will be bad." A fierce scowl twisted her face.

Arel began replacing the salves, wiping each with a cloth.

"We'll have to pretend everything is as usual. If we tip Lord Thomise off, who knows what he'll do. He's already feeling threatened about what's happening between you and Prince Landry."

"Oh, that." Violette waved an airy hand; although, her pink tinged cheeks gave her away.

"Did I miss something?" Auber asked, ignoring the ugly twist in the pit of his stomach.

Violette's cheeks turned redder. "Prince Landry and I met in the library. I know—not the most romantic place, but it's quiet, and I didn't want anyone watching."

"What happened between you and Prince Landry?" Auber wrenched the words from his mouth.

Violette shrugged. "Prince Landry is pleasant. We get along. But he's a flirt, so I can't help feeling he's got a lot of girls lined up."

Auber, cheered by her lukewarm praise of the handsome prince, pressed for more. "Did Prince Landry mention any kind of agreement or alliance with Luixe?"

Violette bit her lip, shaking her head. "No, but it's still early. I can't rush the prince; it would be off-putting." She pressed her fingers against her eyes, taking a deep breath.

"When are you seeing the prince again?" Auber forced the words out.

"Tonight, Prince Landry is meeting me in the east salon. I've sent staff to keep it locked until we arrive."

Auber nodded, trying and failing to feel happy for the princess and Prince Landry. Violette ate her dinner tray in silence, then spent the afternoon in her dressing room trying on gowns.

Finally settling on a dark blue silk with silver embroidered slippers, she covered herself with her veil and slipped out. Auber settled in his armoire nest, alone with his troubling thoughts. If this alliance with Prince Landry worked for Violette, it could be the best solution for

Luixe. But it meant Auber would be trapped as a frog. Forever. Unless he could find some other candidate to break his spell.

Auber choked down a lettuce leaf. Therese didn't mind living in the pond—Arel had checked on her several times, even delivering bits of food which Therese was completely uninterested in; but Auber couldn't bear to spend the rest of his life immersed in slime and muck. And he didn't want to live without Princess Violette. He pushed the thought away and tried to sleep.

A door slammed.

Hasty footsteps swished across the floor. Auber's head snapped up. Who was that? Arel had left for dinner in the servant's wing, and Violette was meeting Prince Landry. He peeked around the corner of the armoire door.

Violette stalked across the carpet, angry tears glittering on her cheeks.

"Violette?" Auber asked, heart wrenching at her distress.

Violette threw herself into the armchair. "Prince Landry never arrived," she said, sniffing and scrubbing her eyes.

"Landry, surely he sent an explanation?" Auber asked. He thought the Iasian prince was enamoured with Violette.

Violette sniffed again. "No, nothing. How dare he! To me?" Fresh tears hung on her lashes.

"Did anyone else know you were meeting Prince Landry?" Auber asked, his mind snapping to thoughts of Lord Thomise and Sophie.

Violette shook her head. "Not a soul, unless Landry told someone."

"He could have." Auber's voice was reasonable.

"What will I do now?" Violette wailed.

"Send a message to learn if Prince Landry is still in Luixe. Landry isn't treacherous; surely he's got a reason," Auber said.

"All right." Violette rang the bell. When a maid appeared, she murmured her instruction quickly. Within an hour, she had her answer.

Landry had fled the castle.

CHAPTER 16

"Where?"

"Back to Lovan. He left this afternoon because his mother is gravely ill," the messenger repeated what he knew.

Violette kept her expression nuetral until the messenger bowed and left.

"Landry never even told me so I guess I didn't mean that much to him after all." Violette's shoulders slumped, defeat etched in every feature. "What should I do now? I don't have time to approach another suitor. Without the Iasian's, we'll never be able to defend ourselves against Lord Thomise."

"It's time you talk to your father," Auber said.

"But with his illness... Are you sure?"

"If someone is plotting against King Abelaird, you need to warn him now."

Violette raised her hand to her cheek. "You're right."

Auber nodded. "King Abelaird's known Lord Thomise a long time, and he'll understand his weaknesses."

Violette smoothed her hands over her dress. "Let's go now before I lose my nerve. And you're speaking too. After all, without you, we'd never have discovered the extent of Lord Thomise's treachery."

Auber hopped into Violette's bag and they went to King Abelaird's study where Violette knocked, waiting patiently. She was only met with silence.

"He's not here. Maybe we should come back later." She turned to leave.

"Try the door," Auber suggested. A niggle of apprehension tickled his spine. Something felt wrong. Off. King Abelaird always spent his afternoons in his study chamber.

Violette grasped the metal handle and turned it, swinging the door open on silent hinges.

King Abelaird lay sprawled across his desk, his face pasty white.

Violette rushed to her father. "Father, are you all right?" she passed a hand in front of his mouth. "He's still breathing."

"Get his tincture," Auber ordered as Violette rushed to do his bidding, dumping the tincture into a glass with shaking hands.

"Father, drink this." She lifted King Abelaird's head, putting the glass to his lips.

King Abelaird stirred and moaned, and Violette managed to get a few drops into his throat.

"Lie down and I'll send for the healer." Violette helped King Abelaird stagger to the settee, where he collapsed, beads of sweat coating his forehead.

"Stay with him and keep him awake," Violette said, setting Auber down before she dashed from the study, calling for help.

"You're still here. I expected Violette to have sent you back to the garden pond by now," King Abelaird muttered, eyeing Auber. The colour was leaking back into his face, and he struggled, sitting upright.

Auber hopped closer to King Abelaird. "Violette takes excellent care of me, but that's not what should concern you right now."

The king threw Auber a sharp look. "Pardon?" he asked, drawing down his brows.

"Your daughter has been trying to save the kingdom. And she's afraid to tell you what she knows. You need to listen and take her seriously."

King Abelaird's eyes glinted. "You're bold for such a tiny creature. But all right, I'll listen."

Violette returned to the king's study, winded and disheveled. "The healer is coming now."

King Abelaird motioned to his daughter. "Come, sit. This creature has informed me you have news? I feel up to hearing it now."

"Are you sure? Moments ago you were.... I thought you were going to die," Violette asked, biting her lip.

"I assure you I'm very much not dead," King Abelaird answered. "Now talk."

Violette took a shaky breath, explaining everything from the time she'd met Auber to Prince Landry's hasty exit.

King Abelaird tightened his lips. "No doubt Sophie and Lord Thomise sent the Prince a false message. We'll worry about that later. First, we deal with the traitor. Unfortunately, we can't arrest him; he's got far too much support."

Violette nodded. "True, we need to find his weakness and strike there."

King Abelaird narrowed his eyes. "Let's take away his support. We might not have much funding, but I have power to lower taxes. Lord Thomise is the one who's been pushing me to raise them. No doubt, attempting to make people unhappy. It's time I took control of my council; I've let them get away with too much."

"Who supports us in the royal council?" Violette asked, leaning forward.

"There must still some council members I can trust, we need to find out who they are and organize a solid plan against Lord Thomise."

"How will we contact them if Lord Thomise has the mirror?" Auber asked the king.

"Ahh.. the mirror Lord Thomise stole from us. We'll take care of that first, leave it to me. And you," King Abelaird said, tightening his lips as he directed the next comment to Auber. "Stay hidden. Something tells me you'll prove to be our best weapon."

Following King Abelaird's direction, Auber accompanied Violette, scar now clearly visible, to the council meeting that afternoon. King Abelaird hadn't disclosed his plan to Violette and Auber about how he intended to regain the magic mirror, but by the glint in his eye, the king looked forward to the confrontation.

Violette arrived in the council chambers early, but kept Auber tucked in the bag. She didn't want to give the council—especially Lord

Thomise— any idea of Auber's usefulness. Auber shifted. All he could see were faint shadows moving across the bag; and he was stuffy and hot. He finally edged above the rim of the bag, watching the council members file in.

Lord Thomise arrived, smiling and jovial. Auber admired his casual ability to spout lies and treachery as if they were nothing. Like his father, Lord Ruben. When they settled and began discussing the orders of business, King Abelaird paused, clearing his throat.

"It was so good of Sophie to let us borrow your magic mirror," King Abelaird said, directing a sly smile at Lord Thomise. "Maybe we can use it to find the excuse for Prince Landry's hasty departure. Poor Violette was making so much progress with the young prince."

"She was? In that state? Er..." Lord Lacalle said, reddening under King Abelaird's fierce gaze.

Lord Thomise's wide smile slipped. "Of course. Sophie is too generous, but I'm afraid her offer was too hasty. The magic mirror has sadly not worked in many years and I'd hate to disappoint you."

"That's no problem. I'll have the court mage examine the mirror. Perhaps there's hope yet. Think how lovely it will be when we return the mirror in working order," King Abelaird said, his smile showing all his teeth.

"Certainly." Lord Thomise's voice was weak. "I'll see if my staff can track it down."

"Oh, that won't be necessary. I'll send one of my men for it this afternoon. Once again, thank you for your generosity."

Auber scrutinized the council members as they absorbed this exchange. A few nodded and smiled, but Auber noted several smiles were tense—forced. He would discuss them with Violette later. Lord Thomise likely had allies in the council, and they were the likely culprits.

Before Lord Thomise could protest further, King Abelaird called for a messenger, sending for the magic mirror. Lord Thomise's throat worked as King Abelaird signed the missive with a flourish and a glint in his eye.

When the meeting adjourned, Lord Thomise didn't linger and rushed off immediately. *Damage control*, Auber thought with satisfaction as he watched Lord Thomise scurry away. The councillors filtered out, leaving Violette and King Abelaird alone.

King Abelaird slumped against his chair, showing for the first time his exhaustion.

"Are you feeling all right, Father?" Violette put a hand to her father's forehead.

"That council meeting took it out of me," King Abelaird admitted. "I'm so careful with what I eat and drink; I don't know what could possibly cause this illness." He dribbled his medicine into his glass and tossed it down his throat.

"You think this illness is not Lord Thomise's work?" Violette asked.

The king shook his head. "No, I'm very careful, and only the steward brings me my food. He fills the plate himself, so if someone attempts to poison me, they'll have to poison the entire castle."

Violette frowned. "Maybe the illness needs to work itself out of your system."

"I think it's actually gotten worse this week," King Abelaird said, eyes drooping. "I'd hate to leave you with the kingdom in this state."

"Don't say that," Violette said, clenching white-knuckled fingers. "You're not leaving me, and the kingdom is going to be fine. We'll lower taxes, make people happy, and reclaim everything Lord Thomise stole. You'll see."

King Abelaird shook his head, heaving himself to his feet. "I'd better go see about this magic mirror. Lord Thomise doesn't know I had it collected an hour before I sent the missive." A sly grin crossed King Abelaird's face. "I wanted to ensure Lord Thomise didn't have an opportunity to rush back before they took it."

Violette put her hand over her mouth and giggled through her tears. "Can I see the mirror?"

"Why not?" King Abelaird shuffled to the door. "Bring your little frog friend too; we're going to my private chambers."

Violette followed her father through the castle, past the king's study to the end of the royal wing corridor.

"Few people are allowed in here," King Abelaird said, fitting a shiny key into a tall door.

Auber's eyes widened as they entered the king's private chambers. King Abelaird certainly lived in luxury. Soft rugs covered the polished marble floors; heavy velvet curtains hung from tall windows. They crossed the threshold into the king's sitting rooms where, against the far wall, leaned an ornate mirror.

"We got this by surprising Lord Thomise." The king admired the shining artifact. "Lord Thomise is too intelligent to let that happen again. We'll have to tread carefully now that he knows we're aware of his treason. This piece had been missing for two generations. No doubt, Lord Thomise's family has been involved from the beginning." The king ran his finger over the jewelled ornament at the top of the mirror. "Shall we try it?"

"How does it work?" Violette asked.

"Hmm.. I'll have to consult the mage," King Abelaird said, scratching his head.

"Stand in front of the mirror and ask it to show you a scene. It needs to be places and people you know."

King Abelaird and Violette shot Auber startled glance.

Auber held up a webbed foot. "I watched Lord Thomise use it, besides, my father was a student of magic and finding one of the magic mirrors was his obsession." he answered with a wry smile.

King Abelaird crinkled his brow. "Your father was a mage, who?"

"Not a mage," Auber explained. "A student of magic with no natural powers or ability of his own. He was obsessed with magic and collected all sorts of artifacts. He made me learn about magic too."

"I see; maybe you could try the mirror first then," King Abelaird suggested.

"All right," Auber said, hopping to the mirror. He grimaced at the sour tang of magic that invaded his senses.

"Show me Lord Thomise," Auber said, looking deep into the mirror, with Violette and King Abelaird hovering close behind him. The mirror cleared, showing Lord Thomise sitting at his desk in his study chamber, gripping a quill. A thunderous expression was on his face, which was purple with anger. He shouted; Auber thought he saw Lord Thomise's lips form the word Sophie.

Presently, Sophie arrived in Lord Thomise's study. Lord Thomise berated his daughter who at first was shocked, but then shouted back, gesturing wildly at her father.

"Lord Thomise will know Sophie's not the leak," King Abelaird said. "But the beauty is, he doesn't know who he can trust now that he thinks someone in his inner circle betrayed him."

King Abelaird's voice trailed away as he sat abruptly in the nearest chair, rubbing his chest.

"Father, are you in pain?" Violette asked, darting to the king's side.

"Fine, just need to catch my breath," Lord Thomise said, closing his eyes.

Auber and Violette watched the king with anxious expressions. King Abelaird opened his eyes again, a tight smile on his lips.

"Shall we find out more?" he asked. King Abelaird looked in the mirror. "Show me the army."

They all gazed at the mirror as the cloudy surface cleared. Someone, Auber assumed the general, judging by the gold chain and medals on his cloak, was giving instructions.

King Abelaird leaned closer. "What is he doing, I thought general Hawkins was down South? That's the city." His brow furrowed.

Violette peered past her father. "That is the city. Look, there are the castle turrets. And look behind the general." She pointed to a group of soldiers milling in the background.

The three watched in silence as the general issued orders to his captains.

"If only we could hear." King Abelaird squinted at the general. "I never was good at lipreading."

"The general is definitely giving orders, and everyone's ready for action. He's got both archers and swordsmen," Auber said.

King Abelaird and Violette exchanged apprehensive glances.

"Lord Thomise couldn't be taking action this soon," King Abelaird muttered.

"Why not?" Auber asked. "He's been preparing for a long time."

King Abelaird gave Auber a searching look. "Did you hear Lord Thomise mention General Hawkin's name while you were at his estate?"

Auber cast his mind back. "Lord Thomise didn't mention the general, but a Lord Hawkins signed expense forms, big ones."

"What were the expense forms for?" King Abelaird asked, narrowing his eyes.

"The forms said logistics, but there were no further details," Auber answered.

King Abelaird pressed his lips together.

"What does that mean, Father?" Violette asked, turning worried eyes toward her King Abelaird.

"It means Lord Thomise is controlling the Luixian army," King Abelaird answered. "He's moving toward the castle. We'll have to lie low because Lord Thomise has General Hawkins in his pocket. But I have my own circle of support. Come. We'll hide here and plan. I trust my steward and my guards implicitly. They'll contact my supporters. Lord Thomise won't find it as easy as he thinks to defeat us."

King Abelaird moved to a carved wooden panel of a hunting scene next to the fireplace and pressed a carved stag horn. The panel swung open on silent hinges.

"What is this?" Violette gaped, peering past her father where the sight of a locked door greeted her.

"My private safety room; I store everything I need here in case of emergency."

"Why didn't you tell me about the safety room?" Violette asked, turning to her father with accusing eyes.

"I should have," King Abelaird admitted, taking a silver key from around his neck. "But you weren't interested in running this kingdom until recently."

Violette lowered her eyes, shame colouring her cheeks. King Abelaird opened the door; scooping up Auber, Violette followed the king through the archway.

Auber expected a rough, dark closet but couldn't have been more surprised. Tiny slits in the wall provided streaks of light that lay in golden strips across the polished marble floor. The room was large, at least the same size as Violette's bedroom. Cupboards lined one wall while the other side of the safe room was fully furnished. Even a fireplace stood at one end.

"We share the chimney," King Abelaird explained, moving across the room to the settee. "We'll be comfortable here until the steward arrives."

"What about the mirror?" Violette glanced at the gaping doorway. "We can't let Lord Thomise get his hands on it again."

With some amount of wrestling, King Abelaird and Violette heaved the mirror into the safe room and leaned it against the wall.

"There." King Abelaird dusted his hands. "He won't get his hands on it now. I actually keep my private treasury in here. Want to see?"

Violette held back a grin. "Yes."

After closing and locking the secret door, King Abelaird led Violette to the row of cupboards.

"This is the most important of them." King Abelaird opened the first door. "The kingdom sceptre. It is our most prized possession. Very powerful so it can't fall into the wrong hands."

King Abelaird lifted a heavy metal sceptre. Its jewelled tip sent prisms of light reflecting across the walls.

"Beautiful." Violette breathed. "What are the stones?" she pointed to the blue stones sparkling at the sceptre. "I've never seen sapphire's that color before."

"They're so ancient, no one knows where they were mined."

King Abelaird wrapped the sceptre in a velvet cloth. "If anything happens to me, protect it at all costs."

Violette nodded, her eyes wide and serious. "I promise, Father."

King Abelaird opened the other cupboards, showing Violette her mother's jewelry. "You'll wear it when your queen." He lifted a gold crown, delicate as lace. "This will be beautiful with your hair. Like your mother."

As King Abelaird replaced the crown and locked the cupboard, a knock sounded at the door.

"The steward." King Abelaird went through the door and tapped out a pattern of raps, which was returned.

King Abelaird unlocked the door, pulling the steward in.

"What's the news?" he asked the steward anxiously. "Has the general reached the castle?"

The steward nodded.

"I want no fighting," King Abelaird said. "Bring me my most trusted advisors. Tiernan and Dukek. Together, we'll find a way to settle peaceably. I am still the king."

The steward nodded. "Will you meet here?"

King Abelaird shook his head. "The council room. Tiernan and I drafted the new taxes already. If we announce them immediately, we'll get citizens on our side."

The steward bowed sharply and departed, his footsteps soundless on the carpet.

"Is that true?" Violette asked.

"Is what true?" King Abelaird turned to his daughter.

"About the taxes. You drew the plans to lower them?"

"I'd been considering it for a while," King Abelaird answered. "Lord Tiernan and Lord Dukek have supported lowering taxes because the burden on the Luixians is too great. We enjoyed such a positive response to lowering the apprentice tax; I thought this could only help the crown, because if the Luixian people gain wealth, we'll gain wealth."

Auber nodded. "It's true, when King Erich and Queen Isabella lowered Lovanian kingdom taxes, their exports improved."

The king threw Auber a considering look. "You seem to know a lot about politics."

"Merely schoolboy lessons," Auber answered, squirming under King Abelaird's intense gaze. "I've never even travelled to Corvan."

"Your family is from Lovanian nobility?" Violette asked Auber.

Desperate to change the touchy subject, Auber scrambled for a new topic of conversation.

"Shouldn't we check the mirror to make sure Lord Thomise doesn't surprise us with his plans?"

King Abelaird agreed; although, his wily expression told Auber the conversation wasn't over. Auber sighed, accepting his secret was on the verge of being discovered. After all, it wasn't like hanging around the castle hoping for Violette to pay attention to him was doing any good. He was nothing more than a talking pet to her.

Together, they moved to the mirror.

"Show me Lord Thomise." The trio peered into the mirror, watching as a new scene emerged in a jumble of hazy shapes. Lord

Thomise appeared to be getting on a horse before the scene jumped and skipped, turning to swirling black.

"What's happening?" Violette asked, squinting at the smooth, blank surface.

King Abelaird tightened his lips. "It appears as if Lord Thomise has warded himself against the mirror. Of course he would have done so. But still, I wouldn't have thought he'd stoop so low as to use dark magic. After all, doesn't he realise the cost?"

Violette paled, lips tightening.

"Maybe Lord Thomise has a cure for the illness?" Auber suggested, not meeting Violette's eyes.

King Abelaird shook his head. "The cost of dark magic doesn't always affect the user. It can jump to anyone from their bloodline, so by using dark magic, Lord Thomise puts his entire family—his entire line—at risk."

Violette bit her lip sharply. "Anyone in the family?" she asked, her voice faint.

"Yes, the entire bloodline, young and old," King Abelaird answered, resting his hand on Violette's shoulder. "Nothing we need to worry about, obviously."

"Obviously," Violette answered, lowering her eyes and fidgeting with the pearls on her dress.

"Let's ask the mirror to show us someone else," Auber suggested.

King Abelaird turned to the mirror. "Show me Sophie."

The scene jumped to the kitchens. It was between meals, so the castle kitchens were deserted and quiet. A kitchen maid scrubbed some dirty pots while another boiled tea and setting out plates of tea and pastry.

"Maybe the mirror isn't working; I don't see Sophie anywhere," Violette said.

"Wait. What's that." Auber pointed to mirror again. "I saw something move near the pastry rack."

They stared, transfixed, as another flash of movement passed in front of the pastry rack. "Sophie must be invisible; she's contaminating the pastries, but how does she know which plates to choose?"

"We use those silver trays for the royal wing." King Abelaird pointed to two silver trays with the Luixian royal crest engraved in the handles. "And we eat different things; Sophie knows I love those cream fish tarts—she's seen me eat them often enough. But Sophie doesn't realize that's the decoy tray. Since my illness, the steward's been delivering one of those wooden trays at random." King Abelaird pointed to a plain wooden tray.

"Still, that nasty little minx," Violette said, narrowing her eyes.

They continued to watch as the mirror's view followed Sophie from the castle kitchens and into her private rooms. Sophie appeared again, sitting at the vanity and combing her long golden hair.

"This isn't actually very interesting," Violette complained, turning away.

"Wait, look at that." Auber pointed as Sophie drew a set of keys out of her pocket. "Aren't those your chamber keys?"

Violette inched forward. "Yes, the old set of keys."

"If you catch Sophie with the keys in her possession, you can prove she's guilty."

Violette's eyes glittered. "She'd have no excuses then."

"If Sophie puts the keys in her pocket, we'll only need the right opportunity to expose her—like at dinner, there'd be plenty of witnesses."

"Dinner, with a castle near under siege?"

King Abelaird smiled tightly. "They can't siege the castle if the doors are wide open. We'll bring everyone, then appear on the balcony to announce we're lowering taxes. Which reminds me, I need to meet Lord Tiernan and Lord Dukek—care to join me?"

Violette scooped up Auber, and they tagged along behind King Abelaird to the council room. The corridors were quiet, hushed conversations halting as King Abelaird and Violette drew near. Even the main salon, usually humming at this time of day, was strangely empty. People knew.

A nervous maid gripping a tray gave King Abelaird and Violette a skittish glance before darting away. King Abelaird kept his footsteps even, but even so, Violette had to skip to keep up with him.

"Is it going to be all right?" Violette whispered as they neared the council room.

"I hope so." A grim expression lurked in King Abelaird's eyes. He threw open the council room door where Lord Dukek and Lord Tiernan were waiting.

King Abelaird gave a sigh of relief.

"Good, the steward found you. This is our chance to change the direction and take charge of the situation. Do you have the papers?"

Lord Tiernan produced a sheaf of parchments. "We've both signed them. All we need is for you to sign and stamp."

King Abelaird scanned the papers; when he was satisfied everything was in order, he reached for a quill, scrawling his signature at the bottom. Then, dipping his ring in the ink, he pressed it firmly below the signature.

"No turning back now; people are gathering. We'll meet on the balcony."

For the first time, Auber noticed the rumble of a crowd gathering outside. Violette went to the window. "How did they all know to come?"

King Abelaird joined his daughter at the window. "Lord Thomise must have used his network to notify them." For the first time, King Abelaird didn't seem so confident in his ability to sway the Luixian citizens.

The crowd wasn't happy. In fact, they were angry.

"Down with Abelaird."

"Down with Abelaird." The chant swelled through the air.

Shivers crept across Auber's skin as he hoped King Abelaird's proposal would be enough to sway the Luixian citizens.

Lord Dukek and Lord Tiernan exchanged uneasy glances. "Do you prefer I make the announcement?" Lord Tiernan offered. "It may be... safer."

King Abelaird straightened the circle of gold resting on his brow. "No, they need to see me. The Luixians need to know I hear them."

King Abelaird and Violette swept down the corridor, flanked by Lord Tiernan and Lord Dukek. The balcony was deserted, the door swinging slightly ajar.

As if they were expected.

A frenzied roar rose when King Abelaird and Violette emerged on the balcony. Auber gulped. The expansive lawn surrounding the castle was packed. Everyone in the city seemed to be there. Soldiers patrolled the perimeter, keeping the crowd in check with glinting swords and grim expressions.

This is more than scattered unhappy citizens; it's a full-blown revolt, Auber thought, eyeing the masses surging below.

King Abelaird cleared his throat, but the crowd was too noisy, too restless to listen.

"Find the trumpeter?" Auber whispered to Violette. Violette darted to the door, reappearing seconds later. The king's steward, Brian, lifted the brass trumpet from a hook on the wall.

"I've never done it before, but how hard can it be?" Brian pressed his lips to the trumpet and blew.

A weak squawk floated from the horn, barely loud enough to hear across the balcony. The crowd below took no notice. Auber watched a burly farmer get into a tussle with a soldier. The situation would spiral out of control quickly if no one made a move.

"Here let me." Violette took the trumpet from Brian, blowing a long clear note. It rang across the castle lawn, hovering over the mutinous citizens. They paused, looking up as one.

Violette let the trumpet fall to her side. "I knew those music lessons would pay off," she whispered to Auber.

King Abelaird stepped to the edge of the balcony, emanating confidence from every fibre.

"People of Luixe, you have been under a heavy burden."

"That's right," a man shouted as the restless crowd murmured in response.

"I have seen your hardship. I and my council have decided to come to your aid and ease your burden."

The unhappy rumbling died down as everyone waited for the king to continue.

King Abelaird held up the new tax agreement over his head. "We have decided to lower taxes."

The crowd mumbled; no one looked happy.

King Abelaird slid an uneasy glance toward Lord Tiernan and Lord Dukek. His grand scheme appeared to have no effect on his unhappy citizens.

"What about the war?" a man shouted. A merchant, judging from his pale skin and rich clothing.

"War?" King Abelaird's confidence faltered as Lord Tiernan and Lord Dukek looked taken aback. "There is no war," King Abelaird raised his voice above the grumbles. "Luixe has always been a peaceful kingdom and will remain peaceful."

The crowd continued to stare at the king.

"No," a man stepped forward.

Lord Thomise.

He climbed on the top of his carriage where he could be seen by everyone.

"King Abelaird is trying to appease you with a few meagre coins. He sits safe in his castle, dining on fine wine and sweetmeats while his people suffer. I say no more. No More. NO. MORE."

The crowd turned to Lord Thomise, ready to whip into a rage, Auber realized. Fists raised in the air as the crowd took up the chant.

No more.

No More!

NO. MORE.

King Abelaird raised his voice again. "Do you think this Lord is different? Will be different…"

The crowd ignored the king, thundering the chant like a song. Something thudded on the balcony, a rotten apple landing just behind Violette. A rock, swiftly followed by another. Then a barrage of objects whistled through the air.

"Get off the balcony," King Abelaird shouted. He grabbed Violette's hand and dragged her inside, slamming the door just as a heavy rock smacked against it.

"That didn't go well." King Abelaird was out of breath as he leaned against the wall, face pale.

"Now what?" Violette twisted her hands together.

King Abelaird's eyes were shadowed. "We need to keep you safe; back to the safe room, immediately."

Followed by Lord Tiernan and Lord Dukek, the group rushed into the corridor, but they were too late. Heavy footsteps echoed against the floor. Lord Thomise's army had arrived.

King Abelaird spun in the other direction as the desperate group raced down another corridor. With a sinking heart, Auber realized Lord Thomise had cut them off. Soldiers were closing in from both directions.

Lord Thomise must have suspected they would come to the balcony.

They were surrounded.

King Abelaird shoved Violette behind him. Lord Dukek and Lord Tiernan drew their swords. "We'll fight for you, my king," Lord Dukek said, raising his blade.

King Abelaird shook his head. "You'll serve me better alive."

Lord Dukek lowered his weapon.

King Abelaird stepped forward to meet the soldiers. Violette cowered behind him until she was jerked forward, a sword at her back. They were roughly tied and dragged to a room on the lower floor.

CHAPTER 17

Tears streaked Violette's cheeks as she slumped against the chamber wall. The soldiers slammed the door. The key grated in the lock.

They were trapped.

"What are they going to do with us?" Violette whispered.

"I don't know," King Abelaird answered, face tight and grim.

Icy claws of apprehension gripped Auber's heart, knowing it was extremely improbable Lord Thomise would allow King Abelaird or Violette to live long. Lord Thomise would leave no holes in his desperate grab at for the Luixian throne.

Violette leaned her head against the stone wall, the scar on her cheek white and bloodless. Auber glanced around, noticing the door was located across the chamber, and King Abelaird, his lords, and Violette were bound too tightly to move.

"Roll over," Auber told Violette, who complied. "Maybe I can untie these ropes."

Auber examined the knots, using his webbed feet to feel along their length. He grunted and fumbled, tugging the thick ropes, but they didn't give. He glanced toward the lengthening shadows, realizing they were quickly running out of time.

Thud thud, thud.

Heavy boots thumped down the corridor; the soldiers were returning. Auber scampered behind a pile of burlap sacks, crouching low to avoid being spotted by Lord Thomise's minions.

Bang, the door flew open.

"Well, well, well," Lord Thomise said, sauntering inside and grinning at the foursome. Five huge, heavily armed soldiers followed him.

Lord Thomise flicked his velvet cape and folded his arms in front of his chest as his sly smirk widened.

"It looks like your little tax plan is a dismal failure." His eyes tightened, although his grin remained wide and toothy. "Although it is unfortunate, I was going to use the tax break to seal the citizen's approval as the next ruler of Luixe." He flicked his eyes over King Abelaird. "No matter, I have other tricks up my sleeve."

"You won't get away with this, Thomise," King Abelaird said, glaring at Lord Thomise. "I am the rightful king; the Luixians know me, and will come to their senses."

"Will they?" Lord Thomise asked, waving a be-ringed hand at one of his soldiers, who snapped to attention. "See no one comes near the royals; I'll keep them alive—for now, we'll need a decent trial—a thrilling spectacle for the Luixian's enjoyment."

Without another glance, Lord Thomise turned on his heel, followed by four soldiers. He strode from the room, slamming the door behind him.

Auber pressed himself against the corridor wall. His heart thudded in his chest.

Exposed.

Although he'd slipped out ahead of Lord Thomise, there were no hiding places in the castle barracks wing. Luckily for Auber, soldiers weren't looking for a diminutive green frog. He watched and listened until their footsteps were hollow echoes on the stone floor.

Auber looked around. The barracks were a part of the royal castle, unfamiliar to him. The walls were solid grey stone, the stone floor uncarpeted. Hoping for the best, he followed the path Lord Thomise and his soldiers had taken.

Legs aching, Auber stopped for a quick rest. He'd dodged and struggled through the castle, but now he was almost at his destination, the servant's quarters. There was a chance he might find a sympathetic servant; perhaps even Arel, if was lucky. Auber crouched behind a wooden barrel in the kitchens to watch to wait.

The kitchens were busy; Lord Thomise must have ordered a lot of food for his people. The room was steamy with the scent of cooking meat and baking bread. Rows of cakes and buns cooled on large metal trays. Auber strained his ears to listen to the kitchen maids as they busied themselves peeling potatoes.

"The commotion would horrify my mother. Ridiculous this carry on, in our day," one of the kitchen maids said, huffing. Her paring knife flicked so rapidly it was a mere blur in her hand.

"I think we're safe in the kitchen," the other kitchen maid said, throwing a peeled potato in a pot of water. "People need food, and Lord Thomise hardly intends to swan into the kitchens and cook."

"What of the other castle staff, how do they fare?"

"Sophie never paid attention to the staff, so they move as they please at the moment. Most staff on the royal wing have deserted the castle—running scared. They're afraid if Lord Thomise tries the king, they'll be liable with the royal family."

"Smart."

The snick-snick of the paring knife paused as the kitchen maid washed another potato to peel.

"A few loyal staff members are staying, taking up other posts. Hoping King Abelaird and Violette return. I suppose with a cushy job in the royal wing, it makes sense to remain loyal. Some are working in the laundry, assuming they won't be noticed in the background."

The kitchen maid snorted. "Unlikely, I heard Lord Thomise has King Abelaird and company trussed up like a chicken the barracks. He'll not get free under Lord Thomise's armed guards."

"True, sad though. Just when King Abelaird's lowering the taxes. If Sophie's anything to judge by, we'd be better off under King Abelaird and Violette's reign. I heard Violette's messy, but lovely to work for."

"I heard Sophie had her maid stand awake by the chamber door all night in case she needed anything." The kitchen maid said, setting down her paring knife and lugging the potato pot to the iron range. "Would you throw the peelings out? I'll get the carrots ready."

Auber shrank back as the maid swept by on her way to the pantry.

The laundry room. Auber took advantage of the open kitchen door to slither into the corridor. He crept into the laundry room, blinking through the steam. The smell of hot clothes and soap hung thick in the air, stinging his eyes. Auber's heart flickered in excitement. Across the steamy room he saw Arel's familiar figure, wringing out the whites into a large metal tub. Keeping to the edge of the room, he crept toward her.

"Arel, Arel," Auber called.

Arel jumped, dropping a handful of hot, soapy fabric with a splat into the sudsy water.

"Auber, you scared me," Arel said, putting a dripping hand to her chest.

"Sorry, I didn't know how else to get your attention. Arel, we have to move fast; I know where King Abelaird and Violette are," Auber whispered, glancing around.

"Come outside, we can speak safely there," Arel whispered from the side of her mouth.

She picked up a basket of wet clothes. "Just going to hang these out," Arel announced to no one in particular as Auber hopped in the basket, hiding underneath a wet tunic.

Arel set the basket next to the clothesline in the courtyard. "Where are they?" she asked, shaking a wet tunic before using the wooden clothes pegs to pin it to the line.

"They're in the barracks, with Lord Dukek and Lord Tiernan."

"But how can I free them?" Arel asked, hanging up a shirt.

"Is your Uncle Morem in the mage guild?"

"I think so," Arel answered, wrinkling her brow. "I never asked him. Why?"

"I have a plan."

CHAPTER 18

Arel drew her cloak over her head and clutched her satchel to her chest as she slipped outside the castle gates.

"Halt, where are you going?" a soldier whipped out his sword. Arel froze in her tracks.

"They sent me to the market for Mistress Sophie; they ran out of the liquorice tea she likes," Arel answered, fluttering her lashes at the soldier.

"Wait there, don't move," the soldier said, frowning. Tense moments dragged by as the soldier whispered with his superior. Eventually, the soldier gave Arel a terse nod and opened the portcullis.

The deserted city streets rang with silence, an interesting change after yesterday's riotous crowds. Arel's footsteps echoed on the cobblestones as she wound through the quiet lanes.

The mage market was subdued; most stalls were empty, abandoned by their venders and merchants as they waited for more stable times. Arel trotted through the stalls, arriving at Uncle Morem's spot. She rapped sharply on the ramshackle wooden table.

Uncle Morem emerged, yawning and smoothing his wild hair and dishevelled clothing.

"Arel, I wasn't expecting you so soon. Here for some more salve? I take it the price wasn't too taxing for Princess Violette."

"No," Arel answered, wrinkling her brow in thought. "Princess Violette hasn't noticed the cost at all."

"Hmm, interesting." Uncle Morem muttered, smoothing his ragged coat. "Well, if you're not here about the salve, what brings you? Hardly a social call in these times, I'd wager." A gold tooth glinted as Uncle Morem grinned.

"King Abelaird sent me; he wants a favour."

"Oh ho, fancy pants king needs me, does he?" Uncle Morem said, hopping on his table, and sitting cross-legged.

"Er, yes, King Abelaird was hoping you could find him a mage."

Uncle Morem raised an eyebrow. "Look around, dear; of course I know mages, but what kind of mage? King Abelaird must want something specific. Is the castle mage too mainstream?"

"The castle mage defected," Arel answered. "Now Uncle Morem, pay attention. We need someone powerful, showy—someone loyal who can wield." Arel leaned close, wrinkling her nose at the rank smell drifting from Uncle Morem's grimy cloak. "Someone who can wield the royal sceptre." She glanced around as she whispered the last word. However, no one was paying any attention to the nondescript maid and the eccentric old mage.

"Hm," Uncle Morem said, seemingly unimpressed. "Etienne might help the king."

"Etienne, is he here today?" Arel asked, scanning the deserted market.

"No, Etienne doesn't need to peddle his wares at the market." Uncle Morem hopped off the wooden table, slinging his ragged satchel over his shoulder. "I know where he lives though; since there's no business here today, I'll take you to him."

Arel, carrying Auber, followed Uncle Morem as he wove through the stalls until they burst out into the blazing sunlight, blinking after the dim light of the market. Uncle Morem strode through the empty streets, leading them to the edge of the city.

"Is this Etienne trustworthy?" Arel asked, hesitating before a modest cottage. A pair of goats grazed in the front yard, neat piles of firewood were stacked beside the cottage.

"Yes, although a bit late to be asking now," Uncle Morem said, swinging the wooden gate open. The goats bleated at the intrusion, alerting a man who emerged from the cottage.

"Father?" the man drew his eyebrows together. Dressed in the rough blue linen of the tradition Luixian farmer, sleeves rolled up to reveal brawny forearms.

Arel stared at her uncle, mouth dropping open in shock. "Your son, when did this happen?"

Morem shrugged, rare hesitation flickering through his eyes. "It's a long story."

Arel nodded, face displaying unanswered questions.

"What brings you here, Father?" Etienne leaned against the shovel he carried, unsmiling; Arel noticed Etienne didn't invite them in.

"Oh, er, Etienne, this is your cousin Arel. She works in the royal palace, and she needs your help."

"Help who at the palace?" Etienne asked, thinning his lips.

"Maybe it would be better if Arel explained herself," Uncle Morem said, giving Arel a little shove.

"Certainly," Arel said, swiping stay strands of hair from her face. "Maybe we should go inside the cottage where we have privacy."

Etienne led them into the cottage, silently opening the door and waiting as they filed into the cottage. Auber peered through the fabric, taking in his surroundings with interest. The cottage was plain but clean, with no curtains, no cushions, no rugs. The furniture was worn, but cared for. Uncle Morem lowered himself into a wooden chair by the hearth.

"It's been a long time since I've seen you, Father," Etienne said, shooting Uncle Morem a hard glare.

"Very busy at the market, you know," Uncle Morem answered, sliding his gaze away.

"Well, we're inside, so what is it you need?" Etienne said.

In a few words, Arel explained the plan.

Etienne listened impassively as Arel spoke, his only reaction a faint twitch in his jaw. "You're crazy, mad, it must run in the family," he answered, glaring at Uncle Morem.

Arel slumped in defeat.

"So you can't help?" she said, her voice small with defeat.

Etienne scratched his chin, letting the uncomfortable silence hover over the tiny cottage room. "Who's that?" he said, breaking the silence and pointing at Arel's bag.

Arel opened the bag, allowing Auber to poke his head out.

"A frog?" Etienne said, staring at Auber. "Who did this to you?"

"My father," Auber answered.

A strange expression flitted across Etienne's face. "Fine, I'll do it. Who knows... maybe I'm crazy too," he said with a sigh, throwing calloused hands in the air.

A brilliant smile lit up Arel's face. "You will?"

She jumped up, embracing Etienne. Etienne froze, slowly putting his arm around Arel's back and patting awkwardly.

"If you're going to do this, we should leave immediately. Lord Thomise will not wait long before the trial, not after King Abelaird's just announced the taxes being lowered." Uncle Morem eyed the cousin's reunion with a sidelong glance.

Arel drew back. "Of course."

Etienne took a few moments to tell the neighbors he was leaving and asked them to milk the goats and feed the chickens before he locked the cottage.

"You inherited your magic from your father?" Arel said, trying to make conversation as they set off toward the city centre. The castle loomed, dark and foreboding against the late afternoon sun.

"Both." Etienne's answer was short. He looked straight ahead, footsteps eating up the road with long strides. Arel trotted to keep up with her cousin.

"Your mother was a mage?" Arel asked, panting.

"Yes," Etienne answered, not glancing for Arel or Uncle Morem.

Uncle Morem remained silent, his discomfort clear on his face; his ragged cloak fluttered behind him in the chilly breeze.

Arel wisely chose not to delve any further into the subject. They drew close to the middle of the city. The city was eerie— deserted marketplaces, streets empty save the soldiers occupying every corner. Lord Thomise must have hailed troops from every outpost.

They slipped unhindered through the winding cobblestone lanes, staying away from principal thoroughfares, drawing ever closer to the castle looming in the center of the city.

"Here's the turnoff to the mage market," Arel said, pausing at a narrow alleyway.

Uncle Morem pressed his mouth in a tight line. "You don't think I'm going to let my niece and son face this alone, do you?" he said, striding ahead.

Arel shrugged, following Uncle Morem.

"How will we get into the castle?" Etienne asked.

Arel froze; it was a reasonable question. It was one matter for a servant to slip out to perform a necessary errand, and quite another to return with two strangers in tow, especially one who looked like Uncle Morem.

"Why don't you go through the garden gate?" Auber suggested. "We can tell Therese the latest developments and ask if she's heard anything since yesterday."

"I can help," Uncle Morem said, grinning as he slipped his hand in his pocket, producing a green glass jar stoppered with a cork.

"What that?" Arel stepped back, suspicion flaring in her eyes.

"This one's harmless; I'll absorb the cost myself," Uncle Morem said, cradling the jar in his grimy hand. "If the gate's guarded, I'll use a tiny pinch. Just enough to slip by the sentries."

Arel pressed her lips together, but there didn't seem to be any other options, so she nodded.

The castle grounds teemed with soldiers. Archers lined the battlements. Arel led Uncle Morem and Etienne to a little used side gate.

"Halt, tell me your business," a soldier said, drawing a gleaming sword, a grim expression on his face.

Uncle Morem's hand flashed inside his ratty cloak as he flicked his fingers at the soldier, spattering him with tiny flecks of muddy sludge.

"What's this?" the soldier glared at his uniform. He wiped a few droplets of the brownish green liquid from his cheek.

"Sorry, my mistake, I got something sticky on my fingers," Uncle Morem said, wiping his fingers on his cloak.

The soldier frowned. "All visitors must report to the main gate." He gripped his sword.

"Certainly," Uncle Morem said, smirking. "But you see, we're here to do the gardens. We were ordered to use this gate."

The soldier blinked, the pupils of his eyes flickering with uncertainly. "Oh, the garden."

"So we'll just go through here," Uncle Morem continued, staring very hard at the soldier.

The soldier took a hesitant step back. "Of course, the garden," he repeated as he turned and unlocked the door.

Uncle Morem strode through, gesturing for Arel and Etienne to follow. They filed through the wooden gate before the soldier closed and locked it behind them.

"I can't believe that worked." Arel turned to her uncle.

Uncle Morem winked. "See, I am useful." He drew his ragged cloak around him. "Now which way to the others."

"First the pond, so I can speak to Therese," Auber said.

The strange trio made their way to the pond.

"Therese, Therese," Auber called.

Across the pond, reeds shivered as a trail of bubbles drifted toward them before a green head popped out of the water.

"I was just about to take a nap on my favorite log," Therese said, crawling onto a half submerged branch.

"Therese, we need your help. Have you been listening like I asked?"

Therese's eyes flicked away from the beetle she was watching. "Listening? To the humans? Are you still trying to spy on them?"

"Yes, for word of Lord Thomise," Auber answered impatiently.

"There weren't many humans around today," Therese said. "A shame, sometimes they drop lovely crumbs that remind me of the old days." A fond smile crossed her face.

"Therese, I'll bring you all the pastries you want if you just focus."

Therese snapped her eyes back to Auber. "Of course most of the humans are quite silly; they only talk about dinners, dresses. The masked ball was all I heard about for weeks," she said, rolling her dark eyes. "There was one human girl who seemed different though."

"Different, how?" Auber asked, his ears perking.

"She would disappear sometimes. One minute she'd be here, the next minute she wouldn't; she's strange."

"Sophie," Arel said.

"That's the girl we want information about. What did she say?"

"She met a man here once, and they were talking about money and jewels. Where they were going to store them and how to transport them safely, that sort of thing."

"Where were they storing the jewels?" Auber asked.

"She sewed them into her dresses. They had another house; one they didn't live in. I think it's Lord Thomise's wife's estate; she inherited it. They're storing the gold there too—coins and whatnot."

"Do you know the estate's location?" Auber asked Arel.

"No, but we'll find out."

"Thanks, Therese, I'm doing everything I can to get us out of this situation, I promise."

"All right," Therese answered. She'd already lost interest, her eyes darting after a buzzing fly. "Don't forget my pastries, I like the strawberry ones best."

The three left Therese and crossed the castle gardens. Usually occupied by strolling visitors, the gardens were empty and the east salon door was locked and barricaded, so Arel had to take them to the kitchen courtyard.

"Can you carry this?" Arel pointed at a wooden casket leaning against the castle wall.

Etienne threw Arel a confused look. "It's a disguise; I'll tell them you're delivering it to the barracks." Arel explained. "Then Uncle Morem can slip in behind us."

Etienne nodded, hoisting the casket on his shoulder. Arel strode confidently toward the kitchen door, taking off her overskirt to reveal her servant's uniform underneath.

"Delivery for the kitchens," she called out, motioning to the soldier guarding the door.

The soldier narrowed his eyes.

"Who ordered this delivery?"

"Lord Thomise himself," Arel answered, her voice cool. "And he won't be too happy if it doesn't arrive."

The soldier eyed them suspiciously but stepped aside to let them pass. Uncle Morem's frail figure bowed under the weight of the cask. Arel swept regally past the soldier with her nose in the air, gesturing for Uncle Morem and Etienne to follow her through the door. Still bearing the casket, the four of them proceeded, unhindered, through a series of narrow servant passageways leading through the heart of the Luixian castle.

"We're getting closer," Auber whispered. They were approaching the barracks. Soldiers loitered around the corridors, occasionally giving the small group the side-eye, but Arel seemed so confident, so sure of herself, that they almost allowed the group to pass unhindered. Not yet.

"Halt."

Arel stopped, glancing at the tall soldier blocking her way. His sweeping cloak, decorated with a gold embroidered insignia, told them he was in charge. That, and the air of authority that emanated from his sharply chiselled features.

Arel bobbed a curtsy. "Yes, my Lord," she said, fluttering her lashes.

"Who ordered this?" the soldier pointed at the cask, raising a dark eyebrow.

"Lord Thomise. He wanted it immediately, for you know... the important meeting?" Arel's cool confidence faltered under his fierce gaze.

"Meeting?" the soldier thinned his lips.

"Oh... maybe I wasn't supposed to say anything," Arel hesitated.

The soldier frowned, suspecting he wasn't as far on the inner circle as he thought.

"Would you like me to send it back, my Lord?" Arel asked.

"No. Go ahead, but next time bring a written order," the soldier said, waving them on. "In fact, maybe I should accompany you, just in case." The soldier muttered, falling behind Uncle Morem and Etienne. Auber felt Arel vibrate with tension. The soldier clearly intended to follow them until they safely reached their destination. Auber peeked through the fabric of his bag. Uncle Morem shifted the cask, reaching into his ragged cloak. Hand clenched tight against his side, he muttered and flicked a finger, sending an almost imperceptible spatter of powder toward the soldier.

Nothing happened. At first. Until the soldier blinked, stepping back. "Did you hear that?" his eyes darted toward the square of white light at the far end of the corridor.

"I did," Etienne answered, exchanging a brief glance with Uncle Morem.

The soldier took another step back, whisking his cloak behind him. "See that you return immediately after delivering the casket."

Etienne nodded, white teeth glinting in the dimly lit corridor. "Of course, my lord," he said, dipping his head.

The soldier snapped around, marching toward the end of the corridor.

"Hurry, we're nearly there," Arel said, resuming her brisk pace, tossing a nervous glance behind her.

"How long will that ward last?" Etienne asked Uncle Morem.

Uncle Morem shrugged. "Not long. I didn't get a chance to complete the ward."

They dropped the casket; the three were nearly running now. One more corner and they would reach the chamber where King Abelaird, Violette and two lords were held.

Careening around the corner, they screeched to a halt. Auber's stomach plummeted. The corridor teemed with soldiers; a cluster hovered outside an unmarked wooden door. The door leading to King Abelaird, Violette, and the two lords.

"How will we get past those soldiers?" Arel whispered under her breath as her shoulders sagged.

Auber gulped. He'd expected a few guards but not ten. Lord Thomise was taking no chances on letting King Abelaird and Violette escape. He suddenly realized what a hare-brained plan this was. Of course, Lord Thomise would guard King Abelaird and Violette with his best men. If the royals escaped and swayed the Luixian people, Lord Thomise's plans would be compromised.

Uncle Morem jerked his head at the others and strode on; Etienne following close behind.

"Delivery," Uncle Morem said, striding through the knot of soldiers.

"That door is locked." A burly soldier wearing a captain's insignia stepped forward.

"Good, good," Uncle Morem said, flicking his hand at the captain. "Now do you have the key? They have ordered me to make my delivery here, and Lord Thomise will be furious if I don't get it done. You know how extremely patient Lord Thomise is when things don't happen his way," Uncle Morem added, winking at the captain.

The captain strained his eyes, attempting to focus.

"Oh yes, of course," he said, his voice monotone.

"So if you don't mind, we'll need the key, please." Uncle Morem's hand reached back into his cloak as he flicked his powder over the other soldiers. Soon everyone was covered with at least a few flecks of brown flecks.

Auber held his breath, watching in disbelief as the captain patted his pockets.

"Key, I have the key," the captain said, drawing out a large silver key and unlocking the door.

The three passed through, Etienne and Uncle Morem dropping the cask just inside the chamber door.

"Now, uniforms." Uncle Morem snapped his fingers at the captain. "We need four uniforms, immediately."

The captain shook his head, confusion blurring his eyes. "I don't have extra uniforms."

"That's fine; we'll use yours."

In moments, the captain and three soldiers had exchanged clothes with King Abelaird, Violette and the two Lords turning their backs to allow Violette some semblance of privacy.

"It's a shame this dress won't fit any of you." Uncle Morem bundled Violette's dress under his arm. "We'll just have to take it with us. Come on."

Uncle Morem took the captain's key and locked the soldiers in the chamber. "It will buy us some time; that ward won't last long," he explained, tucking the key into his ragged cloak. "Where to next?"

"We need to get the sceptre." King Abelaird swung his soldier's cloak behind him. "Violette and I will walk in the middle, less likely to be noticed. It's a pity we haven't got more secret passages in our castle. They weren't in fashion when it was built."

"Never mind, I can take you through the servant corridors; I have them memorized," Arel said. She spun, heading toward the nearest servant's door. Cracking the door open, she glanced down the corridor.

"Come on, it's clear," she said, beckoning for the group to follow.

The two lords led the group, marching down the corridor in their soldier's uniforms and looking fiercely down their noses at any servants who looked like they might question their presence.

"We're going to my chambers," King Abelaird instructed. His face was pale and waxy, the strain and pace taking a toll on him.

"Father, do you have your medicine with you?" Violette said in a low voice. Her brow creased in concern as she eyed the beads of sweat gathering on King Abelaird's forehead.

"I've got some in my chambers," King Abelaird answered.

Violette pressed her lips together as they hurried on. An ominous silence lay thick and heavy on the royal wing; only a single serving maid scurried by, eyes lowered as she rushed past the group, footsteps fading in the distance. King Abelaird's door lay ajar, the interior dark and shadowy.

"I'll go first; I have the best excuse for coming here," Arel said, peeking inside. "It's clear." she said, gesturing for them to follow.

King Abelaird headed straight for the fireplace, quickly opening the door. "Follow me."

Lord Tiernan and Lord Dukek's eyes widened as they entered the king's secret chamber. Uncle Morem was the only person who seemed unfazed, casually strolling the perimeter of the room, murmuring under his breath.

"Where's the medicine?" Violette asked, quickly adding King Abelaird's tincture to a cup and handing it to him. He threw it back, his throat working as he swallowed.

"That's better," he said, taking a deep breath.

"There's a lot of magic in this chamber," Uncle Morem said, returning to the group who'd gathered in the luxurious seating area.

King Abelaird nodded. "There are certain things too valuable for the treasury. They're kept here." He heaved himself to his feet and went to the cupboard. "Here it is." The king opened the cupboard and drew out the velvet covered sceptre. Uncle Morem watched intently as the king uncovered the shining object.

"The Luixian Kingdom sceptre," Etienne said, drawing closer. The sceptre flashed, reflecting light, tiny prisms dancing across the floor and ceiling.

"Unfortunately, the last person in the royal line to carry magic was my grandfather." King Abelaird covered the sceptre, but didn't return it to the cupboard. "Which means, although we have the sceptre, we can't wield it anymore."

"Can someone wield the sceptre for you?" Violette asked.

King Abelaird's face grew thoughtful. "Lucie was able to wield in Lovan; Princess Lucie was a commoner and she used the sceptre to defeat Penelope of Iasia. That was before she married Prince Frederich and became the princess. I'm hoping if someone wields it for Luixe, we can defeat Lord Thomise. Of course, our situation is different; magic isn't forbidden in Luixe; there's always the danger of another gifted mage fighting you for it." King Abelaird turned his eyes to Etienne.

"What is your gift?" the king asked Etienne.

Etienne dipped his head, "Aero."

"The power of air," King Abelaird said, his eyes thoughtful. "So simple, and yet so powerful. I know this is a dangerous undertaking, but would you be willing to take the sceptre and fight Lord Thomise? The sceptre will enhance your gift, and perhaps even give you additional powers."

"It would be my honor, King Abelaird," Etienne said, voice low.

King Abelaird took the sceptre and placed it into Etienne's hand. A surge of magic hummed through the room, throbbing and pulsing with a tingling, wild energy.uber gasped, a tingle of shock racing through his blood. The feeling reminded him of something; a memory niggled at the edge of his brain—so long ago he'd almost forgotten it. His mother. He blinked, dragging his thoughts back to the present.

"Now, we need to gather a crowd," King Abelaird said. "I'll need sympathetic witnesses; the more the better."

Etienne chewed his lip thoughtfully. "I don't know about the city folk, but Luixian farmers remain loyal. Especially after you lowered taxes, I know farmers aren't exciting like your fancy court nobles, but they're honest and steadfast and strong."

Lord Tiernan and Lord Dukek exchanged concerned glances. "How will we gather them if we're trapped in here? We would go, but Lord Thomise would throw us in the dungeon the moment we appeared; everyone knows we stand with the king."

"I'll go." Uncle Morem's eyes glinted. "I know all walks of people, and no one notices me—unless I want them to."

"You would do that for us?" Violette blinked back the moisture from her eyes.

"Er—well—it might be nice to be thrown a token coin or two for my troubles," Uncle Morem added with a sly grin. "But of course I will; I can't let Lord Thomise ruin everything; he's been dying to close the mage market for ages."

"Well then, you must let me outfit you," King Abelaird said, rising to his feet. A pained expression crossed his face, and he sank to his knees, clutching his chest and panting.

"Father, are you all right?" Violette knelt at his chair.

"Just a stitch in my side," King Abelaird gasped, the blood draining from his face.

Uncle Morem pierced the king with sharp, beady eyes. "When did the pain start?" he asked.

"I've been unwell for a while, but I thought my health was improving until I recently took a sudden turn for the worse."

"Less than a week ago?" Uncle Morem asked.

King Abelaird lowered his brow. "I think so. Why?"

"I sense magic on you—my magic."

"But I have used no magic."

A thin cry drew their attention as they turned to see Violette's face drain.

"Could the mage price possibly pass to someone else?" Violette asked in a weak voice.

"Rarely, but it's possible," Uncle Morem answered.

"It's my fault." A tear ran down Violette's cheek and plopped onto the plush carpet. "I used that magic to make my scar disappear so Prince Landry would court me." Another tear joined the first, creating two wet spots.

"I'm sure Morem wouldn't have given you anything dangerous—would he?" King Abelaird said, putting his hand on his daughter's shoulder and glaring at Uncle Morem.

"Er…" Uncle Morem stammered, for the first time lost for words. King Abelaird raised an imperious brow.

"The thing is…" Uncle Morem said, grimy hands fidgeting in his cloak. "If someone asks me, I have to give it to them."

"Have to?" King Abelaird said, voice stern.

"Fine, she offered me a lot of gold, and I had debts to pay," Uncle Morem answered, shifting his feet. "There is a cost, but I gave her such a small glamour, I thought it would be minor—a cough, a cold, an aching leg. I never expected for one moment Princess Violette would pass the cost on to you."

King Abelaird sighed, wincing as he rubbed his chest. "When will this cost wear off?"

"It varies." Something on Uncle Morem's face told Auber he was holding back.

Violette sniffed, rubbing her nose. "Varies, what's that supposed to mean. It will wear off won't it?"

Uncle Morem looked as if he would like to flee, but with the secret door locked tight and the key safe in King Abelaird's pocket, there was nowhere to run. "Usually, within days, if the person is fit and healthy."

The two lords exchanged wary glances. "What if the person isn't healthy?" Lord Tiernan asked.

"Then it's complicated," Uncle Morem admitted, rubbing the side of his head. "I'm sorry, I really am. I never expected it to be passed on to someone unwell, or I would have refused the princess."

King Abelaird heaved a sigh. With his face pale and strained, everyone realized the king was suffering considerable pain. "What's done is done. For now, we'll concentrate on getting through today. But, don't be selling any more glamours unsupervised," the king said, pinning Uncle Morem with a stern look.

"Never again." Uncle Morem flicked his eyes toward the door. "I suppose you'll want someone else to gather the people now?"

"No, you're the best person for the job." King Abelaird fished out the key to the inner door.

Uncle Morem flitted out on silent feet, slipping through King Abelaird's chamber like a cat.

CHAPTER 19

They waited all day for Uncle Morem's return. Hours dragged by, until finally, finally, a sound broke the silence.

Thudding feet.

Violette shot out of her seat and ran to the door, pressing her ear against the thick wooden panel, eyes closed as she strained to hear the muffled voices outside.

"They're looking for us," she whispered to the others. "They must suspect father had a hideaway here." Scraping noises told them that the searchers were getting closer to their target.

Auber was grateful for the double door, even by some miraculous chance their enemies discovered the catch for the king's secret panel; they wouldn't have the key for the solid wooden door behind it.

They held their breath, Lord Tiernan joining Violette at the door, eyes intent as he listened to the muffled voices.

"They're posting guards at the entrance to the king's chambers," Lord Tiernan whispered.

"I'd be surprised if they didn't." King Abelaird didn't seem shocked by Lord Thomise's latest move. "They know we've escaped by now, and Lord Thomise knows the sceptre is missing."

Lord Tiernan nodded. "They're searching for the sceptre in your chambers."

Crashing noises leaked through the chamber walls as the soldiers ransacked King Abelaird's chamber in search of the missing sceptre. The searchers became frustrated, and there was a final shouting argument before the chamber door slammed.

More hours passed.

King Abelaird produced dried rations and water from one of the cupboards. They ate slowly, willing the time to pass until Uncle Morem's return. Auber noticed the fading light through the slits in the wall; darkness was falling. Violette fell asleep, her cheek against her father's shoulder, and King Abelaird put his arm around his daughter, his eyes softening as he gazed at her face, relaxed in sleep.

"I never meant for this to happen," King Abelaird said to Auber. "I wish I had done more for Violette, taught her what she needed to live without me, instead of expecting someone else to take care of her. Whatever happens, thank you for your service to Violette and the Luixian kingdom. You've proved to be a loyal and steadfast friend. Although bringing you to Violette started out as a bit of fun, it's one of the best decisions I've ever made. When you 're freed from your curse, you have a place in the Luixian court if you want it."

Auber nodded, overcome with gratefulness at the King's praise. "It was worth every minute," he said as Violette's mouth opened, emitting a tiny snore. Auber smiled. Even in sleep, Violette made her presence known.

The panel behind the secret door groaned, rolling back on oiled hinges. Someone was opening the door. Auber held his breath.

A rap sounded on the thick wooden door.

"It's me," a hoarse whisper said, Uncle Morem.

King Abelaird held the key to Lord Dukek, who raced to the door and threw it open. Auber glimpsed a relieved expression flash across Etienne's face as Uncle Morem hobbled inside, followed by a whirling breeze.

"It's done," he said. All color had leached from Uncle Morem's pale, exhausted face, and dark circles hung under his eyes, his hair stood wild around his face. He collapsed in a chair. "Just need to catch my breath, had to use a strong glamour to sneak past the guards," he said, wheezing.

"What happened, Uncle Morem?" Arel asked, taking her uncle's hand and squeezing tight.

"The royal wing is heavily guarded." Uncle Morem closed his eyes and leaned his head back. Arel rushed to get her uncle a glass of cool water, waiting as Uncle Morem drank slowly, then wiped the stray droplets of water from around his lips.

"The people gather at the castle gates tomorrow morning. That should provide time for country folk to travel into the city; I've convinced guards to let them in," Uncle Morem wheezed. "And I have information for you—important information."

"What's that?" Violette leaned forward, eyes sharp.

"There's a faction of the army—a large faction—that supports the crown. Lord Thomise sent them to the outposts three days before the palace takeover."

"Are they close enough to call back?" Lord Dukek asked, his face lighting up.

Uncle Morem shrugged. "I have sent messages; hopefully Lord Thomise hasn't moved them farther afield." The colour was returning to Uncle Morem's face, but his eyes remained faded and tired; the grooves his his cheeks and foreheard had deepened over the past few hours.

"What now?" Lord Tiernan asked.

"Now we wait," King Abelaird replied.

King Abelaird's secret room was comfortable, even luxurious for two or three people, but with seven, it quickly grew cramped. After a supper of yet more dried meat and stale bread, they lay on the carpet and couches and attempted to sleep. Auber crept onto an abandoned cushion in the corner, listening to the gentle snores of King Abelaird. Uncle Morem and Etienne whispered in a nearby corner, their voices carrying to Auber's makeshift bed.

"Are you all right father?" Etienne's voice sounded strained.

"Funny, that's the first time you called me that." Uncle Morem answered dryly.

"Well, it's not like you were ever around." Etienne answered, shifting.

"Etienne, your mother and I—things were complicated between us. Her father hated me, eventually I thought it better if I stayed away, for your sake."

"Grandfather's been gone for years old man."

Uncle Morem sighed. "You're right, I should have come back. I'm a coward."

"Fine, I'm glad your back." Etienne's tone lost some of its bitterness. Auber turned his head, as Etienne returned quietly to his sleeping spot, leaving Uncle Morem to stare out the window in silence.

Rustling woke Auber in the middle of the night. The candles had burned out, leaving the room cast in pitch darkness. Thick clouds obscuring the moon meant no light filtered in from the window slits. However this may have affected human eyes, it didn't affect Auber. His amphibian eyes saw everything in precise clarity. He turned his head, searching for the source of the rustling. Nothing obvious indicated anything out of the ordinary. Auber narrowed his eyes, focusing on the far side of the chamber, a shadowed area near the cupboards.

Something moved. A cupboard door squeaked. A slender female figure dressed in breeches and a form-fitting tunic was investigating the contents of the cupboard, searching for something.

Auber squinted, blood chilling in his veins. Arel and Violette had both been wearing dresses. Metal scraped against metal; the figure froze, jerking its head up. To Auber's left, Violette stirred, mumbling, before falling back asleep again.

Auber tapped Violette with his webbed foot, hoping she would respond. Across the chamber, a flash of silver glinted as the intruder slipped a shining dagger into its hand. Auber gulped, remembering one of King Abelaird's cupboards held a collection of weapons. He shook Violette again, desperately hoping he could wake her without alerting the intruder. Violette threw an arm over her face and snored.

Auber couldn't wait any longer.

"Intruder, someone breeched the door," Auber shouted.

He stared in shock as the figure disappeared into thin air. Sophie, she'd followed Uncle Morem when he returned from his errand; that was the cool breeze he'd felt wafting in afterwards.

"What, where?" Etienne asked, the first to respond. He fumbled for his tinder as he shouted. Lord Tiernan and Lord Dukek jumped up, stumbling into each other and falling to the floor in a tangled heap.

In moments, Etienne lit a spare candle and swung it around the room, searching the shadows for the intruder.

"She's invisible," Auber said. "I saw her over by that cupboard, the one storing the weapons."

"Fan out, we'll feel for her," Lord Tiernan said. "Everyone, grab a weapon. Violette, you stay here and keep safe."

Violette rolled her eyes. "I'm not helpless; I've had more training than you have," she said, grabbing a deadly sword and brandishing it. The group fanned out, each person holding a weapon in front of them and waving it back and forth at their invisible opponent. Auber dashed out of their path, crouching under an armchair to avoid the swishing swords.

The awkward group crossed the entire chamber without a single hit.

"She must have circled round," Lord Dukek said, turning from the solid stone wall.

Auber gasped as chilly hands dragged him from his hiding place.

"Put your swords down or your pet dies." The sharp point of Sophie's dagger dragged across Auber's skin.

"She's got Auber," Arel cried, her eyes wide with fear.

Auber struggled and wriggled, but Sophie merely tightened her grip. "That's the last time you destroy our plans, you vile creature," she said, glaring at her prisoner.

Sophie sat in the armchair and crossed her legs. "Anyone comes an inch closer and I'll put my dagger through his neck. Now, lower your weapons." Her voice was calm. Auber squeezed his eyes shut as cold metal bit into his thin skin. The little group exchanged glances, and with a nod from King Abelaird, lowered their swords.

"What do you want?" King Aberlaird asked.

Sophie smiled, a cruel tilting of crimson lips. "That's more like it. I actually want a lot of things—but we'll start with the sceptre. Where is it?"

"The sceptre isn't in this chamber," King Aberlaird said. Violette threw her father a horrified look, then nodded slightly as a thread of communication passed between them.

Sophie lowered her brows. "Then where is the sceptre."

"In the throne room, there's a hidden compartment in the wall," King Abelaird said. "If you want it, I'll take you to it. I'm not sure it works anymore though."

Sophie pressed her lips together. "I'll be the judge of that."

Auber threw the king a desperate glance, wondering what King Abelaird planned to do.

"All right, but I'll need you to guarantee Violette's safety and the safety of everyone in this chamber, then we'll go together."

Sophie raised an eyebrow, her firm grip on Auber unwavering. "You think my father's going to let you go free—just like that?"

"He will if he wants the sceptre. No need to quibble over titles. Violette can go live in our country estate; no one needs to know."

Violette opened her mouth as if to protest, then closed it again at a stern look from King Abelaird.

Sophie sniffed. "There's twenty guards outside the door waiting for me; how am I supposed to accomplish this?"

King Abelaird smiled, a friendly, open smile that gave Auber a glimpse of the leader he must have been before grief and illness struck him. "You're a clever girl, Sophie; you'll find a way. It doesn't matter about me; as long as Violette's unharmed."

"I'll do my best," Sophie said, reluctance in her eyes.

Auber wondered what King Abelaird was playing at. Although he was grateful King Abelaird would spare him, the king couldn't possibly think Lord Thomise was planning to let Violette live; Lord Thomise was too canny to risk the princess returning to claim the throne later.

"Don't you dare hurt him," Violette said, glaring at Sophie, who returned her fierce expression with a sly smirk.

"Oh, I'll leave your little pet alone if you do exactly what I say," Sophie answered. She glanced at King Abelaird. "Well, are we leaving?"

King Abelaird sat on the settee. "I couldn't find the hidden compartment in the dark; I haven't used the panel in ages; we go in the morning."

"But..." Sophie protested.

King Abelaird motioned for the others to join him. "You heard me," he said, lifting the point of his sword ever so slightly. "Remember, you're outnumbered with a mere frog for protection."

After four long, uncomfortable hours, faint light seeped through the slits in the wall, black sky melting to dim, filmy grey. Sophie grew restless, fidgeting with her blade, coming dangerously close to nicking Auber's delicate amphibian skin with her weapon.

Finally, King Aberlaird stood, face haggard and hair askew. He caught his breath, barking out a ragged cough.

"Father, are you all right?" Violette put her hand on the king's shoulder.

"Need my medicine," the king said in a hoarse voice. "In the cupboard." He pointed to where the sceptre had been placed. Violette nodded, a glint of understanding flitting across her features. She headed to the cupboard. Just as Violette reached her hand inside, Lord Tiernan dropped his sword with a noisy clatter. Sophie whipped her head around, giving Violette the chance to slide the velvet covered sceptre into her pocket before Sophie turned back.

"I don't see it," Violette said, making a show of hunting through the cupboard.

"Oh silly me, I laid it on the side table. Do you mind?" King Abelaird directed the comment to Sophie, who nodded with an annoyed huff. Violette snatched the tincture from the table and took it to the king, who dribbled a few droplets directly into his mouth, swallowing them with a grimace.

"Let's go." The king motioned for Lord Dukek to unlock the door for Sophie.

Still clutching Auber in her fist, Sophie swept through the panel, leading them through King Abelaird's chamber. Sophie hadn't been lying about the guards; nervous and grumpy from King Abelaird and Violette's previous escape, they clustered around the King and his entourage as they strode through the corridors for the audience room. Auber didn't recognize any of guards; Lord Thomise was taking no chances that King Abelaird's personal guards would remain loyal. He wondered where the personal guards had gone— locked in the dungeon with the steward, no doubt.

"Wait here with them," Sophie said, her imperious voice echoing through the hall as she directed the phalanx of guards. "I'll go on with the king." She jerked her head for King Abelaird to follow, her soft shoes silent and catlike, swishing across the expansive marble marble floor.

King Abelaird headed for the far side of audience hall; a door there led directly to the castle gates.

So that's his plan, Auber thought. The king wanted safe passage to the castle gates. Sophie followed the king, not loosening her tight grip around Auber's soft middle. King Abelaird paused at an intricately carved wooden panel near the door, pretending to hunt for a latch.

"I need light. Can I open this door? I can't find the catch," the king asked Sophie, an apologetic look on his face.

Sophie frowned before nodding, glancing back to ensure Violette and the others remained well guarded. King Aberlaird unlatched the door, flinging it wide, to let a thick stream of light flood the hall. King Abelaird turned and looked behind him, nodding.

Etienne stepped forward, flinging his arm up. A bolt of light erupted from the sceptre as it flared to life, throbbing in response to the magic in his blood. A metallic taste filled the air with buzzing energy.

"You tricked me."

Sparks of rage shot from Sophie's eyes. "Well, don't just stand there—grab it," she shouted at the guards, who stood frozen in disbelief. "Secure the princess, and whatever you do, don't let go."

Before Sophie finished speaking, a violent wind whipped through the audience hall. The heavy curtains flew through the air and ripped off the windows with its fury. Violette's hair whisked around her face like a silken cloud. Even the most burly of the guards swayed against its power.

Sophie gasped, her hand still clutching Auber in a relentless grip grew cold and clammy. The wind swelled, icy and cold.

"You won't get away with this," Sophie said, hardening her features in spite of the slight tremble in her voice. "My father's arriving soon; your little breeze won't bother him."

King Abelaird smiled, raising an eyebrow. "How is your father going to deal with the crowd at the gate? Listen."

Etienne let the wind die down; Auber strained his ears, hearing for the first time a commotion at the gate. Shouting and chanting.

"We want the true king. We want the true king."

Sophie's face paled. "What have you done?"

Violette shrugged. "I don't know who those people are."

Sophie narrowed her eyes in response, "You'd better not. Remember, I can disappear at any second. I might not be armed now, but that's a problem easily solved."

Violette gulped, taking a hasty step backwards.

"Is that so?" Uncle Morem stepped forward. Reaching a grubby hand into his ratty cloak, he flung it out, spraying Sophie with a muddy liquid.

Sophie glanced down, confusion in her eyes.

Uncle Morem smiled. "That ward, my dear, lets people see your true self." He staggered back, sitting on the marble floor, his face leached of all colour, spent from the price of the magic.

Sophie gasped; Auber felt her hands shake. But she held her ground, tossing her head.

"I still have this." She held up the squirming Auber. "And something tells me he's important to you," she said, throwing Violette a smirk and dancing out of range of anyone who might grab her.

"Violette," the king said, his voice breaking the tension. "It's time." He tilted his head toward the door.

With a helpless glance at Auber, Violette followed her father toward the door.

Sophie let out a furious shriek. "Fine, if that's what you want." She drew her dagger back, slicing through Auber's skin. Black spots swam before Auber's eyes as searing pain flooded every nerve ending.

"No," Violette shouted.

Tearing herself from her Father's grip, she pounced on Sophie, wrenching Auber out of the girl's hands and shoving Sophie to the ground. Instantly, the wind rose, knocking over the guards and whipping around Sophie, trapping her in it's center until Lord Dukek and Lord Tiernan were able to pin her arms to her side, twisting a curtain tie around them and pulling it tight.

"Are you all right?" Violette asked, her voice fading as Auber felt his strength slipping away. "Auber, come back to me." Violette cradled him in gentle hands, tears running down her cheek.

Suddenly, everything flashed to white as intense pain sucked Auber into a vortex of sensation, stretching and pulling his body apart.

****

"Auber?" Auber's vision cleared. He looked up. Violette peered at him, shock etched on every feature.

"What happened?" Auber blinked, his arm stung furiously, a trail of blood leaked from a jagged wound in his arm.

Arm?

Auber stared in shock at his decidedly human arm.

"What did you do?" He looked into Violette's face.

"I don't know." Violette blushed. "I can't talk to you when... your.... your..."

"When I'm what?"

"You're naked." Violette's cheeks flamed.

"Oh." Auber glanced down, realizing he wasn't wearing clothes. Lord Tiernan quickly flung Auber his cloak, which he hastily arranged over himself. When he was covered, Violette gulped as her eyes travelled over Auber's face, taking in the strong jaw, wavy brown hair and green eyes. Auber had inherited his height from his mother, and he was strong with a wide muscular chest leading to a narrow waist and strong legs.

"I don't know what happened," Violette said, hastily changing the subject. "I saw her," she jerked her chin at Sophie, "cut you with the knife and I was so scared and angry that I couldn't think straight."

"You saved me from her," Auber answered. He glanced at Sophie, who was trussed with curtain ties, along with her guards. She squirmed under his gaze, throwing him an angry look.

Violette blushed, staring at her hands. "I didn't know you were so.. so..."

"So what?" Auber held his breath, his eyes searching Violette's.

"Come on, you can discuss that later; the crowd's getting restless," King Abelaird urged, breaking the moment.

Auber suddenly realized the shouts of the crowd outside had swelled to a thundering roar. He glanced at Lord Tiernan's cloak, uncertain how well it would cover him.

"Here." Uncle Morem threw Auber a faded linen tunic and a pair of worn breeches he pulled from his bag.

Auber quickly wriggled into the clothes, the breeches were short and tight, but at least he was covered; then followed King Abelaird as he led the motley group toward the gate.

"How will we get outside?" Lord Dukek asked.

Guards manned the castle gates, and it took at least two full grown men to swing the heavy iron door open. Fortunately, the commotion in the audience hall had gone unnoticed by Lord Thomise's supporters, but this scenario was unlikely to last long. They needed to move fast if they wanted to open the gates and let the crowd inside.

"Etienne?" King Abelaird turned to the mage.

"Be careful son." Uncle Morem said, giving Etienne an encouraging nod.

Etienne raised the sceptre, sending tendrils of wind breezing across the courtyard, startling the guards clustered at the castle gates. In seconds, the wind slid the bolt across, and the gate creaked slowly open. The guards shouted, pressing and shoving against the gate, but their efforts were useless. The force of Etienne's wind overpowered them, dragging them back.

Once open, the Luixian citizens surged through the gates, crowding the courtyard and shouting their chant.

"We want the true king! We want King Abelaird!"

King Abelaird climbed to the top of the wall and stretched out his hand in a regal gesture.

"Look, there he is!" a burly farmer pointed at the king. The news spread through the turbulent crowd; heads turned, focused on the king.

"My people," King Abelaird said, raising his voice to be heard across the wide courtyard. "Thank you for your loyalty and your strength in these troublesome times. You are the flesh and bone of the Luixian kingdom and I owe you my gratitude."

Silenced by the king's words, the crowd stared, waiting.

"The kingdom of Luixe faces difficult times. Our enemies seek to take the crown from me and my daughter—your future queen." He beckoned for Violette to stand beside him. She rose proud and tall, letting the crowd see her true face, scars and all.

An angry rumble spread through the crowd. King Abelaird raised his hand for them to listen.

"You, the Luixian people, decide the fate of the Luixian kingdom. But know this; he who holds the sceptre holds the crown."

Etienne walked through the crowd, holding the sceptre high above his head. The crowd parted, letting him through, whispers of awe threading through as they gazed on the glowing sceptre.

Etienne stood between King Abelaird and Violette. "I wield this sceptre for King Abelaird." He pointed the sceptre to the sky. A wind whistled upward, responding to his command. Auber watched as dark clouds hovering above the castle whipped into a swirling circle.

"We want the true king. We want King Abelaird."

The chant thrummed louder.

King Abelaird nodded to Etienne who clutched the gleaming sceptre tight and closed his eyes in concentration; a sharp blast of wind wheeled beneath the king's feet, thrusting him into the sky. Silenced, the crowd gasped in openmouthed astonishment as King Abelaird rose higher and higher. He landed gently on the balcony overlooking the courtyard. The astonished crowd cheered as King Abelaird smiled.

"Soldiers, are you with me or against me? Join me now and your betrayal will be forgiven." King Abelaird directed his comment toward the guards, who until now had been too confused to react.

"I'm with the true king." A soldier stepped forward, drawing his sword and kneeling toward the balcony.

"And I." Another soldier knelt. Others followed, kneeling before the king and offering their loyalty.

"Now, find the traitor; we have business with him. And look to Violette's safety, the future of the kingdom is with her," King Abelaird said. His smile disappeared; his eyes hardened.

With shouts and cries, the soldiers scattered, searching for Lord Thomise. Within an hour they found him alongside of the colonel, attempting to sneak horses from the king's stable. They dragged him kicking and struggling to the dungeon to await trial.

****

Later that day, when events calmed and the castle was cleared, Violette and Auber joined King Abelaird in his study.

King Abelaird leaned back in his seat, regarding Auber with appraising eyes.

"So, you broke the curse? Would you care to tell me what happened to you?"

Relieved to be able to tell his story, Auber explained how his father, Lord Ruben, turned him and Therese into frogs and how the dragons offered to bring him to Luixe to break the curse.

What kind of a curse did you say this was—a love ward?" King Abelaird asked suspiciously.

Violette stared out the window, finding a sudden fascination with the gardener trimming the hedges around the maze garden. Auber cleared his throat, staring at his hands, his heart beating fast and loud in his chest.

"I see." King Abelaird raised an eyebrow. "Your father is Lord Ruben?" King Abelaird asked, changing the subject. "And you're his only son?"

Auber nodded, "Not that Lord Ruben was much of a father, but yes, I'm his only child."

"You know your father was fabulously wealthy. If he acknowledged you as his son, then you inherit everything, the farmland, the estates, and the mines."

"I suppose," Auber said, staring at the pattern on the carpet. He sneaked a glance at Violette their eyes clashing before she blushed and looked away.

Much to Auber's relief, a knock at the door interrupted the awkward conversation.

"Your Majesty." It was the king's steward. Once released from the dungeon, he had insisted on immediately resuming service. "I've brought you this young lady, because I thought you and your guest might be interested in what she has to say. I had to give her something to wear. A gardener found her stark naked, shivering in the pond."

"Theresa, you're all right." Auber's eyes widened as the frog steward ushered Therese into the study, long dark hair still damp with pond water. Auber jumped up and gave her a hug.

"I'm fine, in fact I've never felt better." Therese returned Auber's embrace. "It was like I was sleeping, and suddenly I woke up soaking wet in the pond. Where is this place?" her curious eyes roved the king's luxurious study.

"We're in Luixe. The dragon's brought us here. Don't you remember any of that?"

Therese squinted, "Vague snippets," she answered. "But when I woke up, I had a fly in my mouth, ugh, it tasted absolutely disgusting." She shuddered.

Auber hid a smile; his childhood friend was back.

"Would you like to try one of these pastries instead?" Auber asked, gesturing to the brimming plate of scones, sandwiches, and strawberry tarts at his elbow.

"Thanks, I'm starving." Therese accepted a pastry and took a giant bite. She closed her eyes and chewed, a blissful expression settling on her face. "I have to ask the bakers how they did the crust; it's even flakier than mine." She opened her eyes and peered at the golden crust, examining the flecks of sugar dusting it.

"You bake dear?" King Abelaird asked, amused by Therese's enthusiasm.

Therese puffed up. "Of course I bake. I'm the best pastry chef Lord Ruben had... Your Highness."

"Well, you're welcome to work in my castle kitchens if you like," King Abelaird offered.

"Really?" Therese grinned. "There's nothing I'd love more." She took another bite of pastry, scattering sugary crumbs on King Abelaird's plush rug.

Violette clapped her hands in delight, "Come on, I'll take you to the kitchen." She dragged Therese down the corridor, Auber following on their heels. After introducing Therese to the kitchen staff, Auber and Violette walked through the garden.

"I heard Landry's coming back, apparently Lord Thomise lied about his mother's illness." Auber said breaking the silence.

"That's nice." Violette plucked a gardenia, twirling it between her fingers.

Auber cleared his throat, "I suppose you'll be reconsidering him now... as a suitor. I mean, if he's returning all that distance..." his voice trailed off into an awkward silence.

"Auber, Prince Landry wasn't interested in me—at least not the real me." Violette answered, her mouth turning down at the corners.

"Violette, of course he was, the only thing you changed was a tiny part of your face. Landry of Iasia is an excellent choice for you." Auber continued, the words spilling out of his mouth.

Violette raised her eyes to his, "What if I'm not interested in Landry." She asked in a low voice.

Auber froze.

"What if I'm interested in someone else, someone who does know me just the way I am." Therese said.

A surge of hope shot through Auber's heart. "Do you mean."

"You, I mean you silly. But obviously that's ridiculous, I mean look at you and look at me." Violette said, throwing her gardenia on the ground.

Auber swallowed, hardly believing the words, "Violette, I love you exactly the way you are."

"You do?" Violette took a step closer.

Auber put his hand to Violette's cheek, moving it to stroke her hair. "Of course I do, you're perfect in every way." He put his arms around her slender frame, resting his cheek on her soft hair.

"There you are, I was hoping I'd find you." Rose the daughter of the duchess of Quoralle ran up puffing as she dragged her flowing skirts across the lawn. Her tiny dog squirmed in her arms, and she set it down. It ran off, chasing the ducks back into the pond.

"Violette, is it true, you have to tell me everything. Is this why you've been avoiding everyone." Rose grabbed Violette's arm and dragged her toward the gazebo. Violette cast a helpless glance at Auber as Rose chattered. Auber shrugged, walking away slowly, a fresh seed of hope planted in his chest.

CHAPTER 20

Auber sat in a place of honour at the front of the audience hall, watching the proceedings as King Abelaird held his royal audience beside Princess Violette. Sophie knelt before the dais, with a guard on either side; her head was bowed, but a glint of defiance kindled deep in her eyes.

"Although you were unduly influenced by your traitorous father, Lord Thomise, you were a willing participant to treason. For your punishment, your magic will be sealed and you will be banished from Luixe." A tear glittered as it rolled down Sophie's cheek. Sealed magic was a punishment reserved for the dangerous and most insidious offenders.

"However, because your mother and siblings didn't participate in treason, I will not remove your lands from your future generations on the condition they remain loyal to the Luixian crown. We will allow them to subsidise you wherever you decide to go."

The crowd murmured as the guards led Sophie away. The next day, armed soldiers would escort her to the border, never returning to Luixe.

"That was a wise and generous punishment, darling," King Abelaird turned to Violette, pride shining from his eyes.

Violette shrugged, her lips tilting. "It's not her fault Lord Thomise was a treasonous, disloyal snake. Sophie's young. This will give her a fresh start somewhere new."

"Sensible," King Abelaird said, bestowing an approving smile on his daughter.

After finishing their audience, dealing with horse thief and a dispute over estate lines, there was one more audience to grant. A woman stepped forward alone, hesitance etched on every feature. She bowed before King Abelaird and Violette, her patched skirt brushing the floor.

"I wish to speak to Violette." A slight tremble betrayed the woman's nervousness.

Violette peered down at the woman. "You seem familiar. Do I know you?"

The woman bit her lip. "We were briefly acquainted, but you don't know my name. I'm Matilda." The woman's eyes settled on Violette's scar, now fainter and smoother, without Sophie's interference with the salves. She bit her lip, her eyes troubled. "I'm Matilda, I owned a pastry cart."

Violette's mouth rounded. "It was your cart that..." her voice trailed off.

Matilda nodded, her eyes downcast. "I want to make amends. I have nothing to give, but I offer my services to the crown." Her voice was low.

The crowd stared at Violette, facing the woman who was the inadvertent cause of her disfigurement in stunned silence.

Violette's breath caught in her throat, her face pale as Auber set a hand on her shoulder.

"That accident wasn't your fault, Matilda; it was mine."

The woman glanced up. "But it was my cart, and I was told to stay late then tip the hot oil on you." A tear spilled down her cheek.

Violette gasped. "Who would force you to do such a terrible thing?"

The woman shook her head, "He didn't tell me his name, but he knew you would stop at the village. He said you couldn't resist a sweet. He offered me gold to do it; judging by his dress and manners, someone of noble birth."

The audience held their breath as murmurs of shock and horror swept through the hall. Violette pressed her lips together, a tear running down her cheek.

"How much gold?" she asked.

"Thirty coins." Thirty gold coins—an absolute fortune to a simple pastry maker, enough to open a bakery or buy a farm.

"I couldn't take the money, so I've been working in my father's barley fields."

Violette leaned back. "I accept your offer of service; I believe there is a new pastry chef who needs an apprentice. You will serve under her in the palace kitchens until you pay your debt."

Unshed tears glistened in the woman's eyes.

"Thank you, Your Highness," Matilda said. With another curtsy, she backed away.

With Violette's words still ringing in the air, King Abelaird dismissed court. The crowd dispersed, and King Abelaird and Violette made their way toward the gardens. Auber hurried to catch up. Since the castle steward had assigned him a chamber in the guest wing, he'd seen less of Violette.

Violette turned, smiling.

"There you are. I was hoping you would find us," she said, taking Auber's arm as they strolled through the corridor. "We thought we'd go for a quick walk before the council meeting. Ugh." Violette wrinkled her nose. "I know council meetings necessary, but Lord Savelle does go on about the tax cuts just because he's in charge of the silversmith guild and isn't raking in the extra coin anymore."

"Remember, you 're choosing three new council members to replace Lord Thomise and his allies. Choose carefully, dear. Even with Lord Thomise's stolen gold returned to the treasury, we're still not out of financial trouble yet," King Abelaird said.

"Such a pity Auber can't be on the king's council; he is a lord, after all. The tax cut was Auber's idea," Violette said, batting long-lashed eyes at King Abelaird. Auber's heart flipped in his chest as he gathered all his courage.

"Well, Auber isn't eligible to be a full council member because he's Lavonian not Luixian, but there's no reason Auber couldn't attend council meetings as a Lovanian representative," King Abelaird said, smiling at his daughter.

Auber cleared his throat, feeling his ears turn hot and his stomach twist into a tight knot of apprehension. "There is one way I could become a Luixian," he said, hesitating.

Violette and King Abelaird turned to stare at Auber, Violette's warm hand on his arm tightening, her mouth opening in a tiny circle her eyes wide.

"I could marry a Luixian," Auber suggested, his heart beating fast and loud in his ears.

Violette's eyes widened. "Who?" she choked in a tiny voice, drawing her hand away.

King Abelaird hid a smile as he waited for Auber to respond.

Auber swallowed. "You silly," he reached for Violette's hand again.

"Me?" Violette smiled.

King Abelaird wisely stepped away, giving Auber and Violette some privacy.

"Are you sure?" Violette asked hesitantly, her hand involuntarily rose to her scarred cheek.

Auber drew her hand away, replacing it with his gentle touch. "Violette, you are beautiful and I love you." His hand moved to stroke her long, silky hair.

"Well, I love you too." A tear trembled on the edge of Violette's lashes. Auber leaned down to press a gentle kiss against her mouth.

****

The Luixians were delighted to celebrate the union of their princess with the man who played an integral role in saving the kingdom, and the fact that Auber's extensive lands and mines would now belong to the crown didn't hurt either. Auber's rich inheritance bolstered the Luixian crown's tenuous financial position, creating stability for the economy to recover. After much deliberation, Auber decided not to rebuild his father's Lavonian estate. Instead, he planted vineyards, letting his father's former employees manage them and only asking them to send casks of wine and goods every year for repayment. Sophie fled to Iasia. The last news Auber and Violette heard was she was trying to insert herself into life in Iasian court. With her magic sealed, Sophie would be limited in the amount of damage she could do.

Auber and Violette celebrated a fall wedding, celebrated in the castle gardens. Violette was splendid in a white silk dress so beautiful that Arel had tears in her eyes as she laced her into it. The sun shone through the sparkling air, and laughter and merriment rang from every corner of the Luixian castle. Even the dragons, who Auber invited, performed a fly by, lighting up the night sky with fireworks, rings of coloured fire that awed even the most jaded of noble guests.

"What would have happened if your father hadn't turned you into a toad?" Violette asked. It was evening, and they had gone to enjoy the end of the party from the castle balcony. The crowds still danced in the gardens below, lit by torches and moonlight.

Auber sipped his hot chocolate. "I wasn't a toad; I was a frog. They're very different things, you know."

Violette wrinkled her nose. "Frog then."

"Well, I guess in the end my father did me a favor, because if he hadn't turned me into a frog, I wouldn't have met you."

Violette smiled, fingering the brand new diamond ring flashing on her slim hand. "Just what I was hoping you'd say."

THE END.

Fantasy Romance/Fairy Tales

Free – A Fairy Tale Retelling of Rapunzel mybook.to/free[1]

Brave – A Fairy Tale Retelling of Beauty and the Beast mybook.to/bravekjj[2]

---

1. http://mybook.to/free

2.   http://mybook.to/bravekjj

Strong – A Fairy Tale Retelling of the Princess and the Pea mybook.to/strongkjj[3]

True – A Fairy Tale Retelling of Puss in Boots mybook.to/True[4]

Loyal – A Fairy Tale Retelling of Red Riding Hood mybook.to/LoyalKristinaJJordan[5]

Pretty – A Fairy Tale Retelling of the Princess Frog -

Bold - A Fairy Tale Retelling of Jack and the Beanstalk – Releasing January 2022

Thank you so much for reading this book.I hope you enjoyed reading the story as much as I enjoyed writing it. If you want to hear more about upcoming books Click here to join my newsletter and receive a free copy of **Free – The Retelling of Rapunzel.**

https://storyoriginapp.com/giveaways/c6b9dd42-e7da-11eb-8e9f-43326747b56a

Like all authors, I love honest reviews and find them very helpful. You are welcome to leave one at the end of the book.

---

3.   http://mybook.to/strongkjj

4.   http://mybook.to/True

5.   http://mybook.to/LoyalKristinaJJordan

Don't miss out!

Visit the website below and you can sign up to receive emails whenever Kristina J Jordan publishes a new book. There's no charge and no obligation.

https://books2read.com/r/B-A-KPEO-VOGTB

Connecting independent readers to independent writers.

Also by Kristina J Jordan

The Crown and the Sceptre
Free A Fairy Tale Retelling of Rapunzel
Strong - A Fairy Tale Retelling of the Princess and the Pea
True A Fairy Tale Retelling of Puss in Boots
Pretty - A fairy Tale Retelling of the Frog Prince
Loyal - A Fairy Tale Retelling of Red Riding Hood

www.ingramcontent.com/pod-product-compliance
Lightning Source LLC
Chambersburg PA
CBHW061444150726
47987CB00001B/325